# THE JEWISH HUSBAND

Lia Levi

# THE JEWISH HUSBAND

*Translated from the Italian
by Antony Shugaar*

Europa
*editions*

Europa Editions
116 East 16th Street
New York, N.Y. 10003
www.europaeditions.com
info@europaeditions.com

Translation by Antony Shugaar
Original title: *L'Albergo della Magnolia*
Translation copyright © 2009 by Europa Editions

Library of Congress Cataloging in Publication Data is available
ISBN 978-1-933372-93-8

Levi, Lia
The Jewish Husband

Book design by Emanuele Ragnisco
www.mekkanografici.com

Cover art © by Adriana Pincherle
*Silvia in bianco* (oil on canvas, 1957)
With kind permission of the artist.

Prepress by Plan.ed – Rome

Printed in Canada

# CONTENTS

# PART ONE

# CHAPTER ONE

Tonight, unexpectedly, I've decided to write to you. I probably won't mail it. At least not for now. But if I can bring myself to begin, I know I'll keep writing you, and for a long time.

Maybe you'll read this all in one piece; perhaps these words will never reach you. Fate will determine that, or I will, if I decide to ask fate to lend me some of its power for a little while.

There was a war here. I imagine you know about it.

We lived through a great danger. It seemed as if this time they would succeed in annihilating us. Then everything changed, and in just six days (in fact, that's what they called it, the Six-Day War) we won a dazzling victory.

I know, "dazzling" is a pompous word to use, but that's how it felt.

And so they started seeking us out, phoning, writing letters. They had been afraid for us, and now they felt the need to tell us how relieved they were.

I'm referring to the Jews in other countries, and perhaps not only the Jews.

Till now they hadn't cared much about our state, and even though there were many who spent their lives supporting us, their sympathy remained vague and deeply contradictory.

Suddenly, though, when faced with the threat of seeing us vanish again, swallowed up by the dark waves of history, it suddenly dawned on them how much they cared about us, and about the land that we had looked after, in a sense, on their behalf.

And so there was a flurry of communications and emotional exchanges.

But no one tried to get in touch with me.

It's understandable. No one has heard from me for years and years.

Now I live in the city and I teach in a high school, but during the twenty years I spent on a kibbutz it was easy for me to vanish from the face of the earth, as if I'd been engulfed by a void.

Here, most of the people have no past, and no one is surprised, no one even asks.

Actually, of course, each of those people has a past, and quite a past. But they've left it behind them—each of them back in their own country—canceled forever, roots rotted and reaching futilely for the sky.

That's why no one tried to contact me.

My parents are dead, but like me they lived in this country. It was the happiest day of my life when I managed to persuade them, when I dragged them away from Italy, from your country, before the fury of the gathering storm could strike down on their grey heads.

I couldn't persuade the others, and so they are no longer with us.

Because they are no longer with us, they couldn't try to get in touch with me. For them, of course, I would have made it easy to find me.

In your country, my parents had a hotel. It was called the Albergo della Magnolia. I'm telling you about this because the Albergo della Magnolia was very important—in a sense, fatal—in my life, so you'll hear about it again.

Fortunately, despite the prohibitions imposed by the Fascist regime, my parents managed to sell the Albergo della Magnolia. And so when they left they had a little money. When they got here, my father even managed to find a part-time job, working in a hotel, of course.

My father had a Lithuanian grandfather. So when he was a boy, he heard Yiddish spoken at home, and some part of that stayed with him.

That's why he managed to fit in in this country, and why he was able to find that part-time job.

My mother never could fit in here.

She wasn't a cheerful person anymore, not the way she had been when we lived in the Albergo della Magnolia. Still, it's certainly better to feel sad occasionally than it is never to have another opportunity to feel sad or cheerful or anything else.

So my parents had a little money they'd managed to bring with them from Italy. With what my father managed to save out of his pay from the hotel, they were able to buy an apartment. It wasn't much of an apartment, but from the balcony, if you craned your neck, you could just glimpse the sea.

Now I live there.

When my parents died, they left the apartment to me, and I left the kibbutz.

No, don't misunderstand me. It's not as if I left the kibbutz just because I had an apartment to live in. Things are never quite so brutally simple.

For some time now it had become clear to me that my experience down in the Negev Desert was over. A yearning to teach had come over me. Greek and Latin. Those were my subjects. My subjects from "before."

I haven't retired yet, and my students are fond of me—at least I think they are. They come to visit me in my little apartment and tell me about things, even about their lives outside of school. They are free to stay as long as they want; I live on my own, so they aren't disturbing anyone.

The only company I have is my cat Shulamit.

Shulamit has a prickly personality. She's a little like me. There are times when I can tell that she has no interest in my company. It doesn't offend me; I understand her perfectly. I'm an old man, and she's getting to be an old woman, too.

Still, when we won this war I told her about it. I also explained to her that now we would finally be able to rest the fingers of our hands, or the claws of our paws, on the Wailing Wall in the Old City. And Shulamit listened to me. She even seemed to be contented.

In the beginning, when I lived in my first kibbutz, life was really tough. We had to pry rocks up out of the earth and move them by hand, and we lived in shabby old tents, tattered and covered with patches.

I may not have been much of a pioneer, but I managed to get by.

Back then, I lived with a group of Italians, but no one wasted time talking about the past. The war was raging in Europe, and we had too much keeping us busy.

At the end of the day, I'd collapse exhausted under the canvas of my tent. Sometimes, to relax, I'd read a book by the light of an acetylene lantern. I read in Italian, since that was the only language I knew, except for a very rudimentary Hebrew.

One evening, when I was absorbed in the pages of Proust, the group leader walked in and literally tore the book out of my hands. Then he started to scold me, saying that by reading that decadent and bourgeois book I was offering clear evidence that I understood nothing of the *chalutzistic* spirit. Then he walked out, taking the book with him.[1]

A few days later, I noticed him. He was sitting with his back against the only tree in the kibbutz, and he was reading my copy of Proust.

I don't know why I find myself telling you this story.

---

[1] From *Ha'Chalutz*, Hebrew for "pioneer," the term referred to Jewish immigrants to Palestine working in the Jewish settlements at tasks that contributed to the development of the country as a Jewish homeland. The movement first developed in Russia, in the wake of the pogroms of 1881.

It's not really that important, after all.

I experienced far more difficult moments. For example, when the Arabs had us surrounded, and when I had to learn the specific skill of shooting at chest height.

You want to know the truth, though? I've forgotten about those things. Almost. They're things that happened, and they aren't things that happened to me alone. I experienced them with others.

But I never forgot what happened with Proust. And it's not a bitter memory. Not at all. It's a sweet memory, with just a hint of melancholy.

The guy who took the book away from me went back to Europe while the war was still raging. And sure enough, the Germans killed him.

Those were the heroic times. Then I moved to a different kibbutz.

In the new kibbutz there were no Italians. They were all from Poland and other countries in eastern Europe, but for shorthand I just referred to them as "Poles."

Almost all of them, like me, avoided talking about the past. No one knew who I was.

Only once, a diminutive young man, with a face drawn and lined as if it had been carved out of seasoned hardwood, said to me without preamble, "You don't seem like an *Italki*," then he turned and left. I never could figure out if it was a compliment or an insult, or how the hell he knew I was from Italy.

To tell the truth, I'm not very dark, maybe because of my Lithuanian great-grandfather.

But I never really learned to speak Yiddish, except for the few basic words I used to speak with my Poles.

When I decided to come to the city to live in my parents' apartment, the kibbutz was flourishing. It had changed completely from the pioneer days. That eased my regret at leaving.

I meet other professors frequently, some of them scholars

from other countries. They all express amazement at the fact that I don't live in Jerusalem.

"Really?! Tel Aviv?" they say, with disappointment.

I don't need them to tell me that Jerusalem is a more beautiful place. In fact, Jerusalem is so completely beautiful that there's no room for you to add anything of your own.

Tel Aviv is different; I know that perfectly well. It's a city of straight lines and flat streets . . . and buildings that are nothing more than buildings . . . Tel Aviv *is* Israel.

And I stubbornly set out to seek its individual, modest beauties, as if I were hunting for strawberries in the forest. Now those strawberries belong to me alone; I picked them myself.

I get up very early and, before leaving for school, I walk and walk near the sea, along the streets of Jaffa. And elsewhere. As long as it's by the sea. I think I have a special friendship with the sea.

You see, in this first letter I told you about what it's like here. But that wasn't what I had in mind when I decided to write you.

If I do keep writing, it will be because I want to revive the "before" that I decided to cancel when I first set foot in this land.

I don't know why I changed my mind. Maybe it's because I feel for the second time that I am a survivor, and maybe because in this hot summer of 1967 an image materialized before my eyes. I saw glowing trails arriving from across the sea. I sensed that they were messages of emotion and signals of solidarity with our destiny, racing toward us.

I too want to try to cross over the sea again.

So I'll try. I'll try to tell what happened. But I have to go back a long way to start the story.

# CHAPTER TWO

I have to start with something from my childhood.

I know that the desire to tell others about when we were children is at the very least matched, if not exceeded, by the desire of your audience to ignore you. That is why the process of falling in love is so important. If you think about it, it's the only time when someone is willing to assimilate somebody else completely, including their childhood. That phase passes, of course.

I have lots of things to tell you. I'll do my best to be brief, at least concerning the first part of my life.

You see, my childhood and the story of the Albergo della Magnolia are closely intertwined. It was in that very hotel that everything began. That's why it's important that I tell you about it.

That's where I come from. I was born and raised in that hotel. But not as a guest. The Albergo della Magnolia was my home, in the sense that it belonged to my father, who lived in it with us, his family.

People could never grasp this way of life—Sonia's father, for instance, couldn't understand it, as I'll explain later on. As soon as I told people that I lived in a hotel, they'd give me a baffled stare, and began to think of me as an eccentric and unreliable individual, a vagabond of some sort, a rootless person. I mean, it's one thing to live in a hotel, but being born in one really starts to sound shady.

Nothing could be more mistaken. By nature, I am a homebody, perhaps even a little too attached to certain habits that spring from my deepest interests. It was life that directed gale-force winds at me, uprooting me until I finally blew away.

Let us say that the Albergo della Magnolia exemplified my true essence, the life I lived before the gathering storm broke.

You can't imagine how lovely it was. I don't know if it is still there, and if it is, it may have changed its name. You can go see for yourself, if you like.

You'll find it—that is, if it still exists—in a little street in a quarter of your Rome which in that period had become very popular among the officials of the Fascist regime. I believe that the neighborhood is still pretty much the way it was: winding little thoroughfares, trees that were frequently blooming, and off in the distance the trumpeting of the elephants in the zoo. I wonder how many times you've strolled through those streets . . .

The hotel was named after a magnolia tree that spread its branches up from the square courtyard to the windows of the fifth floor.

To see those glistening green leaves, proud and self-assured, and the white flowers, was one of the joys of our life. The guests unfailingly asked for a courtyard window, and they'd spend long hours sitting by the window.

On the fifth floor, with room 518, the hotel exhausted its function.

At the end of the hallway, though, five more steps climbed upward, covered by a peacock-blue runner, ending at the foot of a door with an oval brass plaque, engraved with a flowing script inscription: *private*.

Behind that engraved word—"private"—was my home.

It was a genuine, full-fledged home, too, with two bedrooms, a cozy dining room, and a tiny kitchen, though it was used only to heat up the coffee and a cappuccino for our breakfast. My mother ordered everything else we ate from the hotel restaurant downstairs.

My mother was a Roman Jewess, descended from generations of shopkeepers specializing in trousseaus and "*Tutto per la sposa*," literally, "everything for the bride," which included white gowns with long trains and veils wreathed with flowers.

One day, she met my father and—at first sight—fell in love with him and with the Albergo della Magnolia.

If I remember correctly, my father started that hotel not many years after abandoning another hotel—in the wake, I believe, of a disagreement with his business partner. That hotel, in turn, he had inherited from his parents. It was located in a spa town in the Veneto.

The hotel in the Veneto had been founded by my Lithuanian great-grandfather, the one I told you about before. After becoming a successful hotelier, he had managed to Italianize his surname, from Katz to Carpi. At least, that is what my father told me.

And so my father was called Attilio Carpi (and my mother, for your information, Fiorella Sermoneta).

As I told you, my mother, Fiorella, had fallen childishly in love with the Albergo della Magnolia. It was her plaything, the passion to which she devoted all her boundless enthusiasm and overflowing energy at every moment of the day.

It may be that when I was born I interrupted her pursuits to a certain degree. You know, when someone is seriously involved in a game, any interruption is an annoyance, a bothersome distraction.

But because my mother loved me, she always let me take part, although in a marginal role, in her passionate pursuit. In other words, she let me play with her a little.

"Now let's order up a spectacular lunch from the restaurant," she would say with a delighted gleam in her eyes, as if she were still playing with dolls and dollhouses.

I didn't mind the way she was. I had no reason to resent it. I don't think that I was ever unhappy because of her focus on something other than me. In a way it was fun. I liked seeing her hurry into the apartment, her curly hair free and unself-conscious, as if it were an expression of her tireless cheerfulness.

I'd see her for a few minutes. Then she'd hurry away again to her tiny back office on the ground floor, where I think she took care of the bookkeeping.

I was never sure whether what my mother did was actually useful to the operation of the hotel. It may be that my father was simply happy to watch her play.

There was only one thing that I missed in my childhood: the presence of friends my own age or classmates to talk and study with.

"You want him to come over to do homework together? Where?" the mothers of my schoolmates would say, their eyes widening in astonishment at the invitation I had extended. "In a hotel! You want me to send my son to study in a hotel?"

Such was their bafflement that they often forgot to invite me to study at their houses.

So you see, the mere fact of where I ate or slept was enough to make a law-abiding, quiet person like me into a renegade, a citizen who for no other reason found that he was set aside from everyone else. So imagine how things were later, when there was a concrete reason for that separation!

The only friend I had in all those years was my cousin Ruben, the son of my aunt Esterina, who was my mother's sister.

Aunt Esterina, unlike my mother, had continued working at the family bridal shops, Tutto per la sposa, and when she had a son, rather than leave him all day in the care of an ignorant nanny—especially when he was old enough to be doing home-work—she was very happy to bring him to study in our apart-ment marked "private."

We didn't go to the same school, and Ruben was one year behind me, but none of those things mattered. Even if we had different homework, at least we could do it together.

Ruben was my cousin-brother. You can't imagine how nice it is to share a life without sharing parents. It's a love without jealousy or conflict, flowing tranquil as a river through a peaceful meadow.

I loved Ruben very much, and I wish you could have met him, but I'm afraid that's no longer possible.

Aside from that friendship, I lived perched on my roost like a bird in a solitary tree.

But from my windows I too lingered gazing at the enchantment of the magnolia tree. My childhood was scented with that yearning and definitive perfume.

The hotel itself was off limits to me. I was strictly forbidden to mingle with the guests because, as they had explained to me, seeing a child running down a corridor undermines the decorum of a refined public facility.

Can I tell you about just one thing that happened? It's just like in my last letter, when out of my whole life as a pioneer I focused, for some reason, on only one single detail: the story of the book by Proust, which was hardly an important event. It is a scene from my childhood that I've never forgotten.

I had ventured down to the fifth floor because I was suddenly seized with an overwhelming desire to lay eyes on a "guest." And I was in luck. Walking down the hall ahead of me were a couple of foreign visitors, and walking between them was actually a little boy.

It was the first child I had ever met in the hotel! While I observed him from a safe distance, creeping along silently behind him, the little boy suddenly turned and stuck his tongue out at me. At me! The only other child in the hotel!

I don't know what took hold of me. I ran quickly toward them, without making the slightest sound, and kicked the boy hard. Then I hid, quick as a flash, behind the green curtain of the broom closet. I knew all the secrets of the hallway, because sometimes the old cleaning woman, Concetta, took me with her when she cleaned the vacant rooms.

The scene that ensued after I kicked the boy was very funny. The boy yelled in pain, telling his father what had happened; then his father ran up and down the hall, finally peering down the stairwell. The father returned, red-faced and angry, saying that there was no little boy anywhere to be found and that his son must have dreamed it or invented it. Then the father and the mother started quarreling too. I couldn't understand exactly what they were saying, but their tone of voice was unmistakable.

There. That's all. Maybe I remember that scene because I wanted to take revenge on the hotel and my mother's love for it. Or maybe, quite to the contrary, I wanted to reaffirm my ownership, my exclusive right to its secret and hidden places. I was the Robin Hood of those hotel corridors.


That's enough about my childhood.

In high school I was very good at Latin, and even better at Greek.

In the course of my life I've struggled with so many personality defects and shortcomings that I can safely state, without fear of seeming conceited, that I really had a gift for Greek. After my first year I could translate any passage without a dictionary, and I could even help the students from the classes ahead of me.

Now you know how much I loved the Albergo della Magnolia, but I did not make it my life's work.

I became a teacher. Yes, I did very well in the public examination. My test scores allowed me to find a position teaching Latin and Greek in a combined grammar school and high school in the city of Rome.

Back then, when the story that I am going to tell you began, I taught fourth and fifth grades in the grammar school, but at the early age of thirty I was ready to make the great leap up to high school.

Last of all, I still need to tell you about the profound and absorbing passion that took hold of me in those years and which—after a very long interval, with the end of one life and the beginning of another, after the violence of the storm and the days of the kibbutz—began to flourish again, and now accompanies my days like a faithful companion.

Pindar. For years, the goal of translating Pindar had marshaled the energies of my mind, and certainly those of my soul.

"It's a challenge," I would reply to anyone who asked me why I had chosen Pindar. They almost always asked me with a hint of amazement in their voices, because almost no one likes Pindar. Nowadays, I correspond with other scholars, and no one is amazed because they are all engaged in the same enterprise. Back then, though, I had to explain and reiterate: "Yes, it's a challenge. I want to make Pindar readable, at last, but without betraying his essence, so complex and enigmatic."

"If that's your idea of fun!" Ruben would reply, skeptically.

Ruben at the time was a lawyer specializing in civil cases, and all that he remembered of the world of classics were a few glimmering and indifferent recollections from our school days.

"Huh," he had tossed out one day, staring hard at me. "Evidently somewhere deep down you miss the Talmud.

"Definitely. To struggle for hours over the hidden meaning of each individual word . . . that's all very Jewish," he had insisted, as if he had suddenly been dazzled by the brilliance of his intuition.

I shrugged in response. My family's Judaism, in contrast with that of Ruben's family, was only a secondary aspect of life, to be accepted cheerfully from time to time, in order to placate Aunt Esterina, and in honor of the memory of my Lithuanian great-grandfather.

Comparing Pindar to the Talmud . . . that was certainly

something I'd expect from Aunt Esterina. And now I was hearing it from Ruben, of all people.

Well, that is the end of the "before" that I wanted to describe to you.

Now I have to return to the Albergo della Magnolia. Because it was there, at the Albergo della Magnolia, on the ground floor, that through the imaginative and creative machinations of life, in my thirtieth year, I met Sonia, one of the sisters of the house of three girls.

CHAPTER THREE

Before I begin, let me explain something. From this point on, various characters will be introduced onto the stage of my story. Some of them you already know—I am well aware of just how well and how personally you know them—but I plan to ignore that fact. I am going to describe these people to you just as I saw them and as I experienced them, and you, assuming that you still want to go on reading my letters, will have to make an extra effort to see things from my point of view.

I'm not sure that this is fair to you, I know only that I can't do it any other way.

Let's get back to us. To the end of 1929, with the *spumante* corks ready to pop, in celebration of the round-numbered new year of 1930 . . .

It hadn't been much of a year, 1929. The Great Depression, the economic crisis tormenting the world, people in America starving to death and people jumping out of windows on Wall Street.

In Italy, Mussolini wasn't doing too badly. You know, in a dictatorship it's easier to take extreme measures, like reducing wages and salaries. Moreover, the government, and this was a good thing, was vigorously working to begin new public works projects. All things considered, we were doing our best to keep our heads above water, and in a way we were succeeding.

You may wonder just what my personal position was at the time with respect to Fascism. I can sum it up in a word, a term that I coined. I wasn't an opponent of the government. I was a "disapprovant." What I mean by that is that nothing or almost nothing that Mussolini and his acolytes were doing met with my approval, if nothing else in terms of taste and intelligence, but my disapproval did not pass the threshold of commitment and action. The idea of active opposition, a more-or-less clandestine resistance, never passed through my mind.

Instead, I had chosen to turn inward, focusing on myself and my studies, doing my best to ignore what was happening in the outside world and avoiding public discussions, much less active involvement.

I can imagine your opinion of this stance must necessarily be a harsh one, but I ask you to remember that at the time nearly all the intellectuals in Italy were behaving in the same way. Later, in the land of Israel, as I told you, I did my best to find redemption for this behavior.

But let us return to that New Year's Eve of 1930.

My parents, in view of the state of the Italian economy, which despite all the government's efforts was still pretty grim, had decided not to organize any special festivities at the hotel. Instead, they had accepted an invitation to the home of some wealthy relatives of Aunt Esterina's husband.

Then came the unexpected development. A group had rented our ballroom for a private celebration.

This piece of news set my father's teeth on edge. He couldn't tolerate the idea of an event taking place in his hotel without him there to preside over it.

In any case, he had always been skeptical about the seriousness of the economic meltdown everyone was constantly talking about. "The crisis," he often said, "only affects certain levels of the populace; the genuinely wealthy aren't suffering a bit." And now he had proof.

My father was always a hardworking, responsible man. That is why he found—and kept—a job even here in Israel.

He was certainly unwilling to step away from his own domain, on that long-ago New Year's Eve, if there was going to be a party on the premises.

A quarrel erupted, the details of which I'll spare you. The only thing you need to know is that in the end, I offered to spend the evening in the hotel in his place, available to deal with any problems that might arise downstairs in the ballroom.

As far as I was concerned, it was an ideal solution. Without lifting a finger, I had a free pass out of an array of obligations, invitations to parties that demanded blithe hilarity, in a roomful of friends or, even worse, relatives and family acquaintances.

You can imagine my mother's objections, such as what kind of young man had she raised if I preferred being shut up at home instead of out having a good time with young people my own age, and so on.

It's strange to think, isn't it, that—even then—my mother had never really considered the question of what kind of child she had raised.

And what kind of young man was I? I was like all the others, really. You shouldn't think of me as a bookworm or the carica-ture of an absent-minded classical scholar who's always walking into streetlamps. I used to go out, I had friends of my own, I went to the movies and to certain parties, at the insistence of those friends, I knew lots of people and met new people regu-larly, in other words, an almost depressingly normal young man.

I had taken a room on the fifth floor of the Albergo della Magnolia, so I could come and go without interference. I only used the private apartment for studying. By now what had once been a dining room had been transformed into a study hall, with two huge desks piled high with books, dictionaries, and papers covered with writing. And there was never anyone in the private apartment. My father and mother only went up there at night to sleep.

I'd even had a youthful love affair—it dragged on for thirteen months—with a substitute teacher. It hadn't been a particularly uplifting experience. It came to an end without me or her (her name was Elvira, I still remember) even thinking it worth memorializing with a word of farewell. It was such a drab relationship that it just fell asleep and never woke up.

As my parents were leaving, my mother—this is once again the New Year's Eve that would usher in 1930—had a last spasm of indignation: "You're not planning to spend the evening with that Pindar!" she had said to me with a sudden burst of suspicion.

Pindar was my mother's personal enemy. She behaved toward that obscure and long-dead individual as if he were a despicable friend of mine who was bound to lead me into trouble, a friendship to be opposed at all costs.

I offered her words of bland reassurance. She had nothing to worry about! It was because I spent so many evenings out wasting time that the idea of being forced for once to stay home had filled me such joy.

And it was only my desire to plunge once again into the pages of my beloved Pindar that had motivated my none-too-altruistic offer.

At last, there I was, perched in the private apartment, with a clearing of silence dividing me from the rest of the world.

I have to explain this to you. That private apartment, perhaps because of the very meaning of the word, gave me the sensation of a secure and fortified nest, far more than would have been the case if I lived, like everyone else, in an apartment overlooking a shared landing.

I wasn't rootless. If anything, I was a recluse.

And it was that very same New Year's Eve, amidst total silence, that I lingered over those verses.

"But in everything is there due measure, / and most excellent is it to have respect unto fitness of times."

Fitness of times. It was perfect. And simple too. Fitness of times . . . the right moment . . . the due measure of things. The secret of life was here.

What need was there to turn the page? You should linger over poetry at length, with humility, as if in prayer.

But in a flash the silence was broken.

"Professor! Professor!" Someone was making a disagreeable racket, knocking furiously at my door.

"Professor!" the young waiter with the ruddy cheeks of a mountain shepherd stammered frantically as soon as I opened the door he had been knocking on.

"There's been an accident in the ballroom. Signor Tiberio said to ask you to come downstairs."

Tiberio was our punctilious maître d'. Nothing that happened in the Albergo della Magnolia escaped his gimlet eye.

I had always suspected that my mother was secretly jealous of him.

Even as I hastily ran downstairs, ignoring the waiting elevator, the idea ran through my mind. That damned raised dance floor.

I was certain that the dais, a raised platform in the middle of the ballroom that had been the obsession of our interior decorator when we had the ballroom renovated (a platform that I had eyed with suspicion), had been the cause of the accident.

A raised dance floor emanating a soft light is just fine if you sit at a table and sip tea, but when there are dancing couples, loud music, and confusion, people forget about the step, a pitfall waiting to catch the unwary.

When I expressed my misgivings, no one took me seriously. Everyone assumes, wrongly, that a scholar has no practical understanding of how things work.

I was right. It had been the dais.

I stood there, staring at the ballroom, with all its grotesque and glittering interplay of light. The orchestra was motionless, as if paralyzed, instruments poised in midair. It looked like an elaborate piece of marble statuary.

At the center of a cluster of people talking loudly and gesticulating agitatedly, a figure lay flat on the floor.

From that direction I could hear a series of moans, interspersed with genuine shrieks of intense pain. Clearly, someone was badly hurt.

What do I remember of that scene? Tiberio, white as a sheet, was attempting with great energy but not much success to scatter the crowd of people clustering around the figure stretched full-length on the floor. Then, the phrase: "Let him through! It's the owner of the hotel!"

The arrival of an authority figure, however vague, had an immediate effect. The crowd fell silent and finally made way.

I recall the scene . . . a blinding revelation . . . the sensation of waves crashing through alternating fields of darkness and light and then steadying, focusing in on a single image.

There she lay on the floor, her features twisted in pain.

She was beautiful.

In her luminescent grey and silver evening gown she looked like a mermaid caught in a net, struggling for survival.

I stood rooted to the spot, unable to breathe. I wonder if you've ever felt anything like it.

Beauty and pain . . . beauty and pain united, intertwined like a pair of serpents to form a whole, a single work of art.

Beauty and pain, shorthand for all of life. First Pindar as a sort of prologue, and now this. The blinding apparition that suddenly introduced me to the simplest and most profound significance of our existence here on earth.

"This is how she'll look, with these lovely suffering features, when she gives birth to our son."

The absurdity of that thought, which had stolen unexpectedly into the center of my consciousness, brought me back to the immediate situation.

"Everyone, please move away," I said in a determined tone of voice that surprised me. "We've already summoned the hotel doctor. In the meantime, please give the young lady some space."

I was continuing to behave in a clear-headed and efficient manner.

I understood that it was certainly too risky to try to lift or move the injured girl, but I was just as sure that she couldn't be left there, in the middle of the ballroom, with the guests, the waiters, and the musicians who—emerging from their paralysis—were swooping through the crowd like drunken crows.

Fortunately, in her fall, the silver girl had landed on an Oriental carpet.

I can still see that grey and pink carpet, with a large peacock at the center.

I quickly assembled a team of waiters and, together, we started sliding the carpet—very slowly and carefully—along the floor to a little drawing room opening off the ballroom.

I sighed deeply as I finally shut the French doors behind me.

That was when another character came forward, a character whom I want to introduce to you, just as she appeared to me in that long-ago first impression.

"What about me? What am I supposed to do?" a tall and elegant young woman was asking me.

For an instant I stared at her in astonishment. Was this a trick of some kind? This young woman's face was an almost identical version—slightly more regular, slightly more precise—of the features of the girl lying on the carpet.

I can still recall every detail of our first meeting.

"Are you her sister?" I asked courteously.

"Yes, I am. How did you know?"

"Well, you resemble one another very closely—in a certain sense," I added after a moment's hesitation.

In a certain sense, you understand? Yes, they were alike, but also very different!

It was as if the silver girl had chosen to become human and descend to earth in the form of a model, accessible to the everyday life of us ordinary mortals, that instead in that taller figure remained somehow chilly and unchanging, that is, an absolutely remote and abstract form.

"In your opinion, did Sonia break her leg or . . . I don't know, something else?" the sister asked me in a relatively neutral tone of voice.

Sonia. I finally knew her name. I had met Sonia.

"I'm afraid she's broken her leg, but only the doctor can say for sure," I responded distractedly.

I was already busily thinking of what I had to do next.

"Come with me," I said quickly to Sonia's sister.

We returned to the ballroom. I was very persuasive. I told the guests that the injured girl was resting comfortably, waiting for the doctor who would be there any minute. And so I suggested that the party resume.

"In a few minutes that clock will strike midnight and we will all celebrate the beginning of 1930," I added with a somewhat theatrical gesture. "I ask you all to dance and drink a toast to your injured friend." Those are more or less the words I spoke.

It worked better than I expected. Deep down, that's all they were waiting for. The orchestra started playing again and in less than a minute the dance floor was crowded.

"What about me?" I had forgotten about Sonia's sister, who was once again asking me, with a hint of annoyed impatience: "What am I supposed to do?" Her tone was not that of a person asking for help or advice, absolutely not. It was more like the tone of a voice of a guest whom a waiter has neglected to seat.

"Stay here with your friends. I'll let you know when the doctor gets here," I ventured to suggest.

I was sure she'd ignore me, but I was wrong.

"That sounds like a good idea," the girl replied in a placid voice, and then moved off with a brisk step, her airy gown undulating as she went. I think it was apricot-colored. I can still see it . . . the gown . . . a handsome, confident stride . . . a blaze of light . . . cries of joy . . . confusion. All now in the distant past.

I had once again closed the French doors behind me and now, incredibly, I was alone with that creature of beauty and pain who was meekly explaining to me Pindar's "due measure of the world."

"Who are you?" she murmured. You understand? Sonia had finally raised her eyes to my face. She was looking at me.

"It doesn't matter who I am," I replied. "I'll stay here with you." The girl seemed to accept and perhaps even understand that incongruous phrase.

When we heard, through the glass panes of the French doors, cries of "It's midnight!" the racket suddenly rose in tone. The childish racket of the inhabitants of the world.

"It's 1930," I said softly, and Sonia replied with a pained smile: "I know." I had grasped her hand, and it seemed to me that she had responded to my clasp.

For now that's where I'll stop.

You see how I'm telling this story, you can see how I still have before my eyes every scene, every color, every phrase, and the clothing, and the carpet, and the frosted glass panes of the French doors. I know why I remember every detail. That was when my life changed.

# CHAPTER FOUR

P eople have some mistaken ideas about passion. People seem to think that when a human being finds himself in the grip of this feverish emotional turbulence he will, so to speak, jump the rails and begin to display forms of behavior that closely resemble pure madness.

Nothing could be further from the truth. At least as far as I am concerned.

I felt clear-headed, very intelligent, and ready to undertake a series of actions that no military commander could have planned out with equal skill.

And that is precisely where the crux of the matter lies, even though while I was inside of it all I didn't understand it at all. The fact is that my logical mind moved along in a channel that ran parallel to that of everyday logic. The transitions were all reasonable and consequential, as were the transitions of my reasoning, but it was the premises that grew out of a senseless and grotesque fever.

I don't want to be unclear. Let me give you an example. When I insisted on sending our doctor every day to the hospital and, later, to the private clinic, to ask about Sonia's condition, I failed to understand that this excess of zeal sprang entirely from my anxiety to stay in touch with her in any way that I could. No, in my mind I felt confident that this was simply the right thing to do, since we had in some way been responsible for the accident.

Until finally one day the doctor rebelled, firmly declining to go back to a clinic where there was already a substantial staff of physicians and no one required or desired his services.

That first night, New Year's Eve, our doctor had been very skilful in immobilizing the fractured leg before calling the ambulance; and he had boarded the ambulance with the girl, remaining with her at the hospital while she was being admitted and cared for.

At my request, he had also asked Sonia's relatives for her name and address, so that we could immediately file the forms with our insurance company to reimburse her expenses.

And so the doctor felt he had done his duty, and then some. To continue to pursue the case would have been ridiculous and humiliating.

My father intervened in the argument between me and our doctor. "I understand that you are still shocked by the accident; it happened right before your eyes, after all. But I do think that your concern is excessive," he said to me, more or less in those words, and then asked me to forget about it, to stop thinking about it.

But his words did not persuade me. Relying upon my new and powerful logical skills, I had begun to insist, reminding my father that the address of Sonia's family was Via Borgelli 11 (Via Borgelli 11! You can imagine, I repeated it to myself a thousand times a day), and therefore it was in our neighborhood, and that it was a very important thing to preserve our reputation, especially in our own neighborhood, and that the raised dance floor was our mistake, and so we were deeply at fault.

My father looked at me with a slight expression of annoyance. My sudden interest in the reputation of the hotel disconcerted him and, more than anything else, disquieted him. He had long since become accustomed to seeing me distracted, slightly mitigated by an effort to appear courteous, whenever he tried to explain some problem of hotel management to me.

He answered me brusquely, reminding me that our neighbors had no need of a hotel (Wrong! Wrong! They might have guests!) and that there are raised curbs on sidewalks, but that doesn't mean that people spend their lives breaking their legs on them.

You see what I mean when I talk about apparent lucidity? Not only did I think I was right, but I thought I was far more intelligent and perceptive than my father.

For example, I had not hurried out to visit Sonia myself, but instead I had cunningly arranged all those visits by our doctor, so that no suspicion could possibly attach to me.

After a few days, though, my logic suggested to me that I might have gone too far in the opposite direction. Since it was I who had seen to the girl's care, and had spent midnight alone with her until the New Year was rung in, courtesy demanded that I go to visit her at least once to see how she was doing.

And so there I was, with a bouquet of flowers (I had never bought flowers in my life) knocking at the front door of the Villa Giacinta.

I remember that it was raining that day and that the water, pouring off of my umbrella, had bathed the outer leaves of my awkward corsage; it suddenly therefore appeared brightly colored and vivid, pearling with raindrops.

The rain struck me as something wonderful, as did the glass-paned front door of the Villa Giacinta and the bespectacled nun who smiled at me as if she'd been waiting for me all her life.

It was my second meeting with Sonia.

That is why I have to tell you about it. You will see yet other characters step onto the stage. I beg you to be patient. Perhaps this is just a weakness of mine, but I feel the need to introduce you to them in the same order and context in which they appeared to me, that is, in a orderly progression through time and through my memory of that time.

Soon, I believe, the stage of our personal theater will be complete and we will be able to speak only about what happened.

In order to remain faithful to this maniacal sense of the order of my memories, I have to take a small step backward. This will serve to introduce one of those characters whom we left, so to speak, behind us.

Yes, we need to return for a moment to the scene of the accident, when Sonia, beautiful and suffering, was still stretched out on the grey and pink carpet, awaiting the arrival of the doctor.

As we were there, still waiting, a young man appeared, dressed in an impeccable tailcoat and an even more impeccable mustachio. He seemed very agitated. He had begun to inveigh against us because the doctor had not yet arrived, demanding in a louder-than-necessary voice why the doctor didn't live right there in the hotel, and other things of that sort.

The funny thing was that as this young man raised his voice, our good doctor, plump and unruffled, was right behind him, and in less than a minute had already set to work.

I later learned that this elegant young man was none other than the fiancé of Sonia's pretty sister, and that he had arrived at the party after midnight, in time to learn of the accident.

"Clotilde," he went on to say with a stern glance, in order to assign to some specific target his fury, which had been left to hover aimlessly. "Why aren't you with your sister?"

And do you know what the tall girl, whose name I had just learned was Clotilde, said to him? "It was him. He told me to go into the ballroom," pointing a languid finger at me as she spoke.

Now let's return to me, in the corridor of the Villa Giacinta, with my bouquet of flowers pearling raindrops, outside of the door of Room 114.

All my confidence had suddenly vanished. Who would I find

inside that room? Certainly not Sonia by herself. Perhaps Clotilde, who might decide to level another accusation against me. Or maybe the mother, or even worse, the father. What kind of a mess had I got myself into?

Even now I can't say whether I was trying to conquer my fear or just overly eager to see Sonia again; whatever the reason, I pounded on the door like a police officer about to enter the den of a dangerous criminal.

My noisy entrance into Room 114 of the Villa Giacinta was the target of much hilarity in Sonia's family for many years to come.

When I walked into the room, I looked only toward the bed. In my mind I had imagined Sonia's figure countless times, but I had always imagined her the way I had seen her on the rug that night.

I was certain that I would find Sonia, in her bed in the clinic as well, still dressed in that silver gown like a mermaid caught in a fisherman's net.

Instead, she looked quite different. She was stretched out, half-reclining on the bed, her back supported by a vast number of pillows, wearing a pathetic little white sleeping sweater, with light-blue crocheted embroidery, terminating in a satin ribbon the same light-blue shade, knotted at the neck like the smock of an elementary schoolgirl.

I remember that I was so petrified in my effort to transform my internal imagery, from silver gown to light-blue sweater-blouse, that Sonia had pointed to the flowers, asking, "Are those for me?" just to prompt a response.

It was not until then that I recovered my composure and made the effort to look around.

Clotilde wasn't there. Instead, there was a middle-aged matron who looked like Clotilde, and who therefore looked like Sonia as well. Another one. In that family, all they seemed to do was pass along the same set of facial features, content to make only slight variations in each one, in accordance with age and personality.

I confess that I felt a moment's irritation, in part because it struck me as an offense to the sense of uniqueness that I attributed to Sonia.

The woman was trying to focus on me, squinting as if she were nearsighted or as if I were somehow dazzling. Whatever the explanation, her gaze was anything but warm. If, as everything led me to believe, she was the mother of both girls, she was much more Clotilde's mother than she was Sonia's.

Now Sonia was explaining to the woman that I was the owner of the hotel, "the one who helped me, who did so much to take care of me," she added.

Her voice was as luminous as I'd always imagined it. That evening on the carpet she had only whispered to me "I know," but even then I was certain that her voice would be exactly the way it sounded now, as I listened to her explain that I had taken care of her. She was speaking to me, not to her mother.

The mother murmured that, yes, of course, Clotilde had told her something about that, but then at the mention of Clotilde her expression had darkened. I wondered: perhaps Clotilde's fiancé had told her . . .

"This is another daughter of mine," she had felt obliged to point out.

I turned my head. I realized how stiffly I had been sitting on the chair the whole time. Only once I turned my head did I finally see "the other daughter."

Another daughter! For some reason, I had felt sure that there were only two sisters.

At the far end of the room sat a dark-haired girl, sitting on a chair, her legs extended as if she were resting. She was more a little girl than a young woman.

I heaved a sigh of relief. At last, here was one who looked nothing like the rest of the family. In fact, she was completely different. Her black hair was bristly, her gaze was direct, her nose and mouth were prominent, perhaps even oversized.

"She looks like Ruben's little sister," I thought to myself in amusement.

To find a discordant note in that family cheered me up, even struck me as funny, as if someone attending a formal business meeting suddenly started to tell jokes.

I immediately felt much more at my ease, and so I pointed out that my father was the owner of the hotel and that I actually had a very different profession. "I'm a teacher," I explained. "I teach Latin and Greek."

"Ah." Sonia's mother showed no increase or variation in interest in me after this clarification. Hotelkeeper or teacher amounted to the same thing for her.

"She studies Latin and Greek, too," she said, pointing to the dark young girl. "She insisted on going to the classical high school, who can say why . . . Perhaps she is one of your students."

"I don't believe so," I said with a smile, "I almost always manage to recognize my students and even to remember them." I rather doubt that Sonia's mother managed to grasp my irony.

"Her name is Lorenza," Sonia broke in, to change the subject.

Lorenza. Even the name stuck out, a bit unusual. Clotilde, Sonia, Lorenza. Having mastered those three names was for me a bit like setting foot inside the house of the three sisters. I almost felt as if I were within reach.

But it was Sonia who threw my life into turmoil.

At last I could speak to her and tell her anything, any bit of nonsense, anyway, it wasn't the words that mattered. In fact, I talked to her about the insurance, and I could see clearly that Sonia wasn't even listening to me. For that matter, I wasn't even listening to myself. Our eyes were speaking words of their own.

And so I hadn't been fooling myself, I hadn't invented a fairy tale that began one New Year Eve. Sonia was exactly as I had glimpsed her that night. In her was the "due measure," the harmony that Pindar had described.

There it was, the due measure, the harmony of gestures, words, gazes, that tranquil way of moving through life, helping everything around her to move more smoothly. A very rare thing.

This was Sonia.

I have a confused memory of Sonia telling me that soon she would be able to go home and that her parents had found her a private nurse.

Go home? How could I get inside Via Borgelli 11? My thoughts wandered, but I wasn't upset. I would see Sonia again, no matter how long she was immobilized in that apartment in Via Borgelli 11 . . .

When it became clear a little later that the time had come to say goodbye, Sonia said to me: "*Arrivederci*, professore." "Arrivederci" meant that she wanted to see me again, and "professore" meant that she liked the work I did.

# CHAPTER FIVE

S onia was about to return home, and it seemed at first that everything was destined to come to an end, the way that most of the illusions and dreams that spring up when we usher in the new year tend to fade away.

I would no longer have any plausible reason to call on her.

Passion however tends to ignore reality, and if it is allowed free rein, it will continue to gallop along fearlessly. Galloping alongside was my unexpected efficiency as a strategist. Yes, I continued to outdo myself.

I had already ventured past Sonia's home in the Via Borgelli 11, more than once. It was a handsome large building, a Roman *palazzina*, yellow ocher with white stuccowork surrounding the windows, and even though there were six or seven families—as I recall—living in other apartments in the same building, it looked like a private villa with a wrought-iron fence wrapping all around it, enclosing a garden that wasn't all that big, but that was beautifully tended.

I will never forget that *palazzina*, and the bougainvillea clambering up the façade, though the first time I happened to walk past it, the branches were still bare and wintry. When the villa's doors finally swung open to admit me, though, the bougainvillea had already burst into a festival of scarlet and red.

I already knew that the Gentile family occupied the entire top floor. I had seen Sonia's mother walk in through the main street door and, once, Lorenza come running out.

I had even spied on their elderly housekeeper. I knew that

she was the family housekeeper because I had seen her walking with a grocery bag on one arm, next to the lady of the house.

One day I sensed that Sonia must already have returned to the yellow *palazzina* to continue her recovery. I received confirmation with a phone call to the clinic, but deep down I was already certain of it. It was as if the windows and the bougainvillea with its flowers as yet unblossomed were emanating vibrations.

Now how could I get to her? That is, how could I communicate with a girl consigned to her bed, with a plaster cast on one leg, whom I could hardly hope to see walking out of the gate in a wrought-iron fence?

The first thing that occurred to me was to write her a letter, but her family would immediately be up in arms, demanding explanations and perhaps even insisting on reading the letter themselves.

But I went ahead and wrote to her anyway. In fact, I had written more than one letter, just to keep from losing a sense of contact with her, but then I placed them all safely in a drawer. I had discarded the idea of handing the letter to a family member, say, Lorenza, or perhaps the housekeeper, because it really seemed a bit absurd.

Then inspiration struck.

The nurse. During my surveillance of the *palazzina*, I had identified the nurse, a fairly young but disheveled woman, who left by the main street door sometime after eight every evening, evidently after preparing her patient for the night.

With the same resolute determination with which I had practically knocked down the door of Room 114 in the Villa Giacinta, I stopped her. Fortunately, I was neatly dressed and I held my hat in one hand in a courteous fashion, and so she got over her initial fright fairly quickly. In fact, I immediately sensed that I had made a good impression on her. I explained to her that I was Sonia's secret admirer, but that her family hadn't accepted me yet. I begged her fervently to deliver my letter to her patient.

I remember that the woman hesitated in a moment of confusion, and I took advantage of the pause to slip the letter and a small sum into her hand.

Over the course of time, we became friends. It was a routine by now. I'd wait for her near the street door, hand her the letter, and she would in turn deliver Sonia's letter to me (yes, she wrote back immediately, and I'll tell you about that shortly), and then I would walk her to her trolley stop.

She would tell me about her life, her misfortunes, sickness in her family, her young children, and their money troubles, but also about falling in love, and how her husband, the best-looking boy in their neighborhood, had chosen her out of all the other girls.

I did my best to help her, but the better acquainted we became, the more reluctant she was to accept money from me. Finally, I began to bring her packets with various provisions and leftover food from the hotel kitchen.

Once she asked me, "Why doesn't the *dottore* want you as a son-in-law?"

"Because I'm only a schoolteacher," I answered her instinctively, confident that she would be appalled. But she seemed to consider it a perfectly reasonable motive. "Of course, *professore* . . . not much money," she responded, rubbing her thumb and index finger together in a meaningful gesture. But then she urged me not to lose heart. "If you can manage to win him over, the *dottore* can find a position for you in his bank . . . He's the bank director, that is, the boss," she told me, suddenly giddy because she was now in the role of giving advice, and therefore, for once, in a position of superiority.

My friendship with Signora Annunziata lasted for the entire three months that Sonia was confined to recovery at home. It's still clearly impressed in my memory, though, as a stretch of courtesy and kindness during that period.

As soon as Sonia recovered, Annunziata vanished from our lives. She did come to see me once at the Albergo della Magnolia, but she was clearly shy and uncomfortable, and didn't stay long.

You see how strange memories can be? I was telling you about how, once we overcame the first obstacles, love was able to flourish and grow between me and Sonia, and I wandered off track to tell you about the poor nurse.

That's what life is like, though. While we are absorbed in major, decisive events, the little things continue to flow and to intertwine, so that years later we have a hard time focusing on the main topic.

Yes, Nurse Annunziata was an integral part of my love affair with Sonia, and there are nights, now that I have forbidden Sonia from returning to my mind, when it is Annunziata who weirdly comes to take Sonia's place in my recollections.

The love that bound me and Sonia together, I was saying, was built, brick upon brick, in that period of Signora Annunziata, with her cheap down-at-the-heel shoes and her fleeting memories of a passionate love of many years previous. It was built on the foundation of the letters that she carried for us.

If life bars the path of a love that has just burst into existence, if a fallen tree crashes down and blocks the trail, then those feelings that would otherwise simply intertwine gradually, floating unhindered on the high and low tides of love, are suddenly compressed into a constricted space. They stop fluctuating; they feed upon themselves until they grow to be enormous.

We had just found one another and then, for a long period of time, we were no longer allowed to see one another. The only bridge connecting two people in love and kept apart by distance was that string of letters, made up of increasingly powerful, feverish words, the very same letters that were delivered (and, in Sonia's case, even written) secretly by a complicit and zealous hand.

In those letters we thought we were analyzing our emotions, and instead we were building them. Anyone would have been thrilled.

But we had the foolhardy certainty that this was more than merely a passing inebriation.

A passion, of course, demands an audience, and I had chosen Ruben as my audience. Ruben was a sober, down-to-earth type, and it had not escaped my notice that he had some serious misgivings. The more heated I became, the more doubtful and hesitant was the expression on his face.

"The thing is, you barely know her," he blurted out one day. "It all strikes me as a mental concoction, it's like the plot of a nineteenth-century novel." Ruben had never been anything other than sincere in his life, at least with me.

I patiently tried to explain to him that love can indeed grow over time, as two people get to know one another better, but that having various interests in common isn't enough. There's something else, something that eludes rational thought, something that belongs to the realm of mystery.

You see, I would tell him, the reverse can happen as well. From the very first instant there might be an explosion of certainty that what will become evident later is already present, implicit, and fully established . . . And what you discover over the course of time, in that case, is nothing more than a confirmation of that certainty.

"Literature, literature," Ruben would mock me. "You don't even know how she thinks, what her opinions are. I don't know, her political views, for instance. What if she turns out to be an enthusiastic proponent of Fascism?"

I understood that Ruben enjoyed provoking me, but I shrugged it off.

Do you know what I thought when he said that? First of all,

I told him that what I had sensed in Sonia made such a thing inconceivable. Second, and at the time I felt no fear about it (and I was wrong), that even if it turned out that matters stood as Ruben feared, I wouldn't have cared a bit.

That then is how I set foot, if only in my thoughts, on the first step downward. A vague thought, on which I didn't even focus with any emphasis, one of those fleeting images that surface for an instance and then vanish in the rush of events.

I even dragged Ruben to see the house in the Via Borgelli 11.

"Why would you think I care about seeing the house?" Ruben groused. Then, to make me happy, he looked up and told me that it was a fine house; since he was still Ruben, he immediately added that he still liked the Albergo della Magnolia better.

Time went by, and even though the idea would have seemed unthinkable just a few months earlier, the moment had come when Sonia began to venture outdoors again, at first accompanied and with a certain degree of caution, and then in a perfectly normal fashion.

In due course, we chanced to meet one day, just as everyone happens to meet when they're out and about. We understood that the period of epistolary exaltation, fed by distance, had come to an end, and now we were about to come face to face with real life. In other words, this was a crucial moment, and it might spell the collapse of everything: that idea was perfectly clear to both of us.

And so we were both nervous and worried. But we were wrong.

Let me tell you right away that meeting, face to face—Sonia standing upright and walking comfortably, dressed in a spring outfit whose particulars may elude me now, though I have a firm memory of the color, a vague sense of pink, that much is certain—instantly swept away any lingering fears.

Once again, it was just like that New Year's Eve, everything flowed spontaneously. And just as on that evening, I once again began to sense that "due measure" and "fitness of times" that manifested itself in the perfect fusion of the features of her face, her voice, her gestures, her glance, in a complete and uncommon equilibrium with the rest of the world.

We began to see one another more often, though still in secret, and to tell one another everything about ourselves, as if we had never written letters, as if those letters had been about other people.

We strolled happily through long sunny days untouched by shadows. Then, one day, by chance, while talking about some unrelated subject, I happened to mention that I was Jewish.

No, I'd never told her that fact, nor had I written it in any of those letters, but only because I considered it to be an irrelevant detail of my life, nothing but a detail, no different from the fact that I had a Lithuanian great-grandfather. I was completely steeped in the attractions of the world of Hellenic culture, and there was simply no space for Judaism in that world of mine.

Judaism . . . Nothing more than fasting on the holiday of Yom Kippur—nothing more than a custom, tradition that had always been followed, who could say why, even by secular and unbelieving Jews (the so-called "Kippur Jews," perhaps you've heard of them)—and the Passover Seder meal at my Aunt Esterina's house. In other words, I was a Jew twice a year, not much to speak of out of 365 days. You should also keep in mind that back then, in 1930, the race laws still lay in the future and that, all things considered, there wasn't much talk about Jews in Italy.

Perhaps you have a hard time believing that my silence was not purely accidental, perhaps my subconscious (though back then we knew almost nothing about the subconscious) feared that revelation as a harbinger of trouble to come and was attempting to ward it off. Who can say? It's certainly all possible. But I can assure you that even now I am inclined to think that my delay in sharing this detail was a result of nothing more than the motives I mentioned, nothing more. Being Jewish wasn't especially important to me, nor to my parents: we were hotel people, international people.

I certainly would never have expected the reaction that followed. Sonia stared at me, horrified, while her face, suddenly ashen, seemed to contract like a muscle being tensed.

"No . . . that's not possible," Sonia murmured as if to herself. "I can't marry a Jew. We are Catholics. My family is very religious. You can't imagine. For them, not being married in church means living in sin . . .

"You can't imagine . . ." she went on repeating, in a sort of monotonous singsong.

I have a fragmentary memory of my agitation, of the bitter taste in my mouth as if I were chewing on iron filings. Yes, that's the only real memory that survives. Aside from that, a limitless sense of astonishment, my inept efforts to say something to her, to calm her down: "We'll find a solution . . . we'll find a solution," though I had nothing specific in mind. And what else?

Oh, yes. Sonia began to cry, even though she had never broken down before, not even when she was flat on her back, with a shattered leg, on the gray and pink carpet of the Albergo della Magnolia.

"My father will never accept this!" Sonia finally cried out, and then ran away as I stood there, helpless, motionless.

It was as if the bridge between the Albergo della Magnolia and the yellow *palazzina* in Via Borgelli 11 had suddenly collapsed, shattering into a thousand pieces.

# CHAPTER SIX

F rom happiness to unhappiness is just a short step, from unhappiness to happiness is a long journey," said the Sages. You see, now the culture of our forefathers is no longer so alien to me. And do you know what I think? It's not all that distant from the culture of the classics in which I immersed myself for so many years. Perhaps because I have the cosmic sense of human suffering and the struggle to live, and I think that in the final analysis this is what our sacred books were telling us about, and the legends of the heathens were about the same thing—whether narrating about the Greek gods or the Pure Spirit of the universe.

We were both very unhappy after I told Sonia that I was Jewish, and she reacted in the way I described.

The idea of building a future for me and Sonia together came to seem like an impossibility at a certain point; then, slowly, we struggled to rebuild. It was a long and laborious process.

At first Sonia decided that it was best not to meet again. She thought it pointless, since it seemed that there was no future in store for the two of us. But we couldn't manage to stay apart; we would find ourselves tripping over our feet in our haste to be together again; and it was almost always Sonia who took the initiative. Then I would watch Sonia move away from me, suffering and tormenting herself with remorse.

You may wonder where the mystery of Sonia had fled, that sense of her inner harmony that had struck me so deeply from the first time I met her. And I have to say immediately that, in the wake of this very brief period of disruption, Sonia had miraculously reemerged, reappearing before my eyes just as I had intuited her.

She had presented the problem to her parents, and was waging the daunting battle all alone. I knew that there had been furious quarrels, prohibitions, clashes, and truces. Sonia told me every detail, and the whole time she preserved that surprising equilibrium of hers.

She talked to me about her parents. It was an odd thing— even though she was fighting with them, whenever she told me in detail about what they had said to one another, I never sensed feelings of hostility toward them, I never heard negative judgments. She simply described what had happened. For instance, the time that Sonia's mother, in an attempt to remember me more clearly, blurted out, "Ah, yes, I seem to recall he was a schoolmaster somewhere." Sonia had laughed, and when she told me about it she laughed again.

Until, one day, she said to me, "There might be a solution," and her voice quavered with excitement. Her face managed to express at the same time unbridled happiness and profound anxiety, a fairly unusual combination.

She told me about the "Pauline marriage," that is, a Catholic ceremony, held in church, where basically the Catholic spouse was given the ritual sacrament while the non-Catholic spouse was present more or less as an observer, keeping his own religious faith with the understanding that they would raise their future children in the Catholic and apostolic Roman religion.

I had already heard some vague mention of this Pauline marriage, but I went to find out more from the priest who taught religion at my school, an enlightened priest who was a close friend of mine. Yes, Don Anselmo explained to me, the Pauline marriage is, all things considered, an honorable compromise that reconciles an array of different needs. "It is a very wise provision of the church," he said, "to have invented such a sophisticated way of bringing people into harmony."

You must be wondering what I felt when I heard this suggestion.

Well, first and foremost, and perhaps solely, an overwhelming joy. That's all. We had found a way around the obstacle, and that was all that mattered. The how and the why were of no concern to me.

Someone had managed to shift the boulder that blocked our path, and I could only rejoice.

That is the truth, the naked truth about what I felt at the time. The impetuous force of our passion was so powerful! Let me tell you again, I would have agreed to anything . . . to rob . . . to kill, I couldn't say. I wouldn't be the first.

I have to add, though, that even in rational terms, if I tried to analyze the matter coldly, I didn't see what was so bad about it. Sure, I would enter a church and I would take part, let us say, apparently as a participant but in reality uninvolved, in a ritual belonging to another religion. I would cause some minor discomfort to my parents, I would cause considerable pain to my Aunt Esterina, but really, all these things were acceptable, or at least, tolerable.

Of the two of us, Sonia was the one who cared about her faith. I had only the mildest attachment to my own faith. There was no injustice, there was no bullying. It was understandable that of the two of us, the one with less at stake would be willing to yield.

I was willing to make Sonia happy and eager to make our marriage possible at an affordable cost. After all, deep down I would only be acting as a curious spectator. I have always been an observer, and being present at a ritual I had never witnessed before struck me as a matter of considerable interest.

I believe that I've been sincere in this account. It is the truth. I wouldn't have any reason to lie at a distance of so many years. My state of mind was exactly as I've described it to you.

"Papa wants to meet you," Sonia said to me one day, and I felt that finally the moment had arrived. I was about to attain the dream I had been pursuing since the evening I first met Sonia. I was about to step over the threshold of Via Borgelli 11.

But that's not what happened, at least not that time. Giuseppe Gentile agreed to meet me in his office at the bank at nightfall, long after the last of his employees had left for the day.

One thing that impressed was the furniture, almost black in color, carved out of solid oak with large leaves, and the sharp contrast with the open window and the mild May weather outside, with birds swooping wildly through the darkening air, designing elaborate and graceful arabesques against the deepening blue of the evening sky.

Then I looked at him.

I had never constructed in my imagination a picture of Sonia's father, perhaps because I had been so impressed by the repetition of the same features and physical type in the mother and the two older sisters, and therefore I was stuck with an odd notion of a sort of specially constructed mold used to produce the members of the Gentile family.

But Giuseppe Gentile had nothing to do with that mold.

Sonia's father transmitted something in his admittedly tall figure that was both massive and imposing, an expression of detached arrogance that seemed to spring more out of his physique than any inner attitude. It was as if his neck had been designed as a device with only one working part, and this prevented him from ever lowering his gaze to the level of ordinary mortals.

Only his penetrating and fundamentally menacing gaze managed in some sense to connect with whoever came into his presence, and that gaze seized hold of his interlocutor, and only reluctantly released him.

In sharp contrast with the rest of his persona was a weak and sensual mouth, which—despite all his efforts—transmitted the opposite message, undercutting in a way that massive deployment of focused energy.

At that moment, Sonia's father was pointing straight at me the imperative gaze that had so impressed me when I first met him. I can't say that he was observing me with hostility, but whatever it was, it wasn't entirely friendly.

He spoke to me in the neutral tones you would use to talk about a piece of business. He seemed like a chess player, already thinking about his next move while making this one. And it was a strange thing that he should work so hard to play against me. He was already perfectly well aware that I had fully agreed to the Pauline marriage.

He talked about various subjects, first about his family, then his deep involvement with Catholic associations, and how pleased he was at the recent official sanction of full compatibility between Catholic Action and the National Fascist Party.

"We are all so impressed with what Fascism has succeeded in achieving for our country, and this recent clarification has finally set at rest the minds of many Italian Catholics. After all, it's only natural: God, Fatherland, Family. We share so many basic values."

It was clear that he had included me in that "We are all so impressed," but I didn't think that he was looking for confirmation from me, that is, I doubt that he was trying to put me to the test. He certainly took for granted my wholehearted enthusiasm for the Fascist regime, and my silence was enough for him.

He went on talking, explaining in minute detail the rite of the Pauline marriage, a rite about which I was by now pretty well informed. After a while I started to wonder what he wanted with me, why he was going on at such length.

"Listen," he said to me with a sudden verbal lunge. "There's one more small favor I'd like to ask of you. You know, I really believe that it's important for children to grow up with as little conflict as is humanly possible, and I hope that is the case for the children you have with Sonia. You agree with me on this point, don't you?"

In some bewilderment I said, yes, of course, I fully agree.

"Fine," he added, speaking a little louder as he did so. "I ask you to give me your word as a gentleman that you will never reveal to any children you two may have together the fact that you are of Jewish descent. It's for the reasons that I mentioned, in order to keep from confusing them, creating conflicts in their minds . . ."

And as I stared at him, speechless, he completed the sentence, this time in a bland and rapid tone of voice: "Of course, this would also apply to our friends and acquaintances. There is no reason for them to know our private business."

Then, before I had a chance to reply, he started to submerge me in another flood of words . . . Carpi was certainly the name of a city, but he wasn't familiar with it as a Jewish surname. And after all, not every surname that was also the name of a city was necessarily a Jewish surname, was it? For instance, the deputy director of his bank was named Palermo and he certainly wasn't Jewish, and the same was true for lots of other surnames . . .

He talked and talked, and I understood that he was doing it to keep me off balance, to overwhelm and submerge my thoughts, to camouflage his second and final lunge, which arrived ineluctably.

"So, you agree?" he asked me, suddenly breaking off his flow of words and focusing his relentless gaze upon me.

I said that I did.

I don't know why I did, or maybe I do know. I wanted Sonia, whatever the cost.

And then there was my confusion, I was thinking so many different things all at the same time—that perhaps we'd never even have children, that I was always free to break the promise, that, who could say, perhaps Sonia's father might die, and after all, what did I care about that tangle of words, all his tawdry maneuvering? I was someone else, someone quite different from him. I was a person with a rich inner world of ideas and culture, I possessed the power of thought, I was someone who—someone who was in love with Sonia.

Giuseppe Gentile, in the short span of time that had passed between when he asked his question and I had replied with my yes, had held me fast, so to speak, like a hunting dog with the prey clamped tight between its jaws, and there was no power on earth that can make it release its grip.

Afterward, he relaxed.

He started asking me about my profession and whether I intended to pursue a university career.

"I don't know about that," I replied with some hesitation. "I still need to take the examination to teach at the high school level." Before I could finish, he waved his hand dismissively, as if to say "Nonsense."

"I have plenty of contacts at the Ministry of Education," he explained, "let's see what we can do to move things along a little."

Then he asked me about my translation of Pindar (he didn't know the name, he just referred to "that Greek lyric poet"), and whether I had already submitted the project to a publisher.

When I replied to that question, as well, my voice was hesitant, uncertain. Actually, all I really cared about was the translation itself—that was my chief source of joy. I hadn't even gotten around to the idea of publishing it.

But Sonia's father was a man who looked for results, and he promised me help in arranging to publish my work without my even asking.

In any case, I mistook his offer of assistance for an act of kindness, a sign of friendship, and I was pleased and flattered.

When I finally found myself outside the office door ("I still have a few matters to take care of," Dottore Gentile had said to me, but it was plain as day that he wanted to avoid leaving with me), I felt dazed; I felt as if I were sliding over the crests of a series of waves.

I didn't even try to think through what had happened or the words we had spoken to one another; it was more than I could do.

The idea that every obstacle standing in our way, separating me from Sonia, had been removed, blazed with such a blinding light that it prevented me from glimpsing any details—what am I saying?—it kept me from seeing any object or any person that was not the image of Sonia.

# Chapter Seven

T alking with my father and mother wasn't as hard for me as I had vaguely feared. I had decided to tell them about the Pauline marriage, but I had also decided that I would keep to myself the other requests that Sonia's father had made during our private meeting. After all, it had been nothing more than a private conversation that, at least for the moment, was not likely to result in any visible outcome. These were nothing more than words we had exchanged concerning a problem that might arise at some future date, or might not.

I must say in all sincerity that at the time I was unable to say—nor can I say now, with the benefit of so many years of hindsight—I was unable to say, I was telling you, whether my parents felt any pain or displeasure when I told them.

My father listened to me amiably enough, though at first he seemed much more interested in his pipe than what I had to say. I was even a little annoyed by his distraction. Okay, smoking his pipe was his way of relaxing when he wasn't overseeing the hotel, but that this conversation should be taken as a moment of relaxation struck me as a bit much.

Then my father suddenly looked up at me with his pale, slightly Nordic eyes, and began to question me closely about the rules and protocols of the Pauline marriage. He asked questions and thrashed out details in that slightly nitpicking manner of his, and it was as if we were reading entries from an encyclopaedia together. That had happened once or twice when I was a child.

In other words, it was as if we were sitting there reasoning about some abstract event that was of no more than intellectual importance.

Then he suddenly fell silent and resumed puffing on his pipe.

My mother, on the other hand, seemed slightly bewildered. After a while, when it became clear that her husband was not going do anything more than smoke his pipe, and that therefore she couldn't expect any help from that quarter, she asked me in a hesitant manner if I intended to convert to Christianity.

I patiently explained that I had no such intentions. I mean, I had carefully spent the past two hours laying out the details of the Pauline marriage and I felt sure that she had understood. Then I said that it would be unlikely for anyone as non-religious as me to turn suddenly into a fervent believer, especially of another faith.

She seemed somewhat relieved, even though the phrase "What on earth will Aunt Esterina say?," which I had expected for a while now, emerged without fail.

But my mother's astonishment was boundless when I expained to her that the girl I had fallen in love with (that I was head over heels with some girl had been clear to her for a while) was none other than the girl who broke her leg on New Year's Eve, when she tripped over the dais in our hotel.

My mother emitted a long "Ohh" of amazement, her lips round and her curls quivering in excitement. I immediately realized that she was beginning to find this story amusing. And that was all.

Once the conversation was over, my parents returned to their customary occupations and from that day forward, as I have said, they never gave me any indication of how they actually felt about our brief meeting in the private apartment of the Albergo della Magnolia. By the way, the magnolia was in full bloom, and through the open window there wafted the scent of my childhood.

But I still wasn't done. I still had to tell Ruben everything. It was logical, it was natural, and inside was a sense of urgency intermittently tempered by a strong sense of apprehension.

I would also tell Ruben about my conversation with Sonia's father. That was the point. Whatever else might happen, I could never keep a secret from my friend and brother.

I would often walk and talk with Ruben, from evening till late at night, up and down the narrow streets in the neighborhood around the Albergo della Magnolia, discussing all manner of things until Ruben missed the last tram and had to walk home. Sometimes I would walk him home, so that I had to cover the whole distance—twice.

My mother, who was always secretly afraid that I had grown up to become an absent-minded bookworm, incapable of taking part in the rites of passage of young people my age, looked favorably upon my evening outings. She surely would never have guessed that, instead of plunging into the excitement of some social event or another, or even the chaotic whirl of a nightclub or bar, I was spending my time in unhurried conversation with my cousin, that is, with the son of my Aunt Esterina. And if my mother had ever found out, she would certainly have been deeply disappointed.

Ruben and I didn't limit our conversations to the progress of our love interests; in fact, in the past, before I had dragged him into the folly of my feelings for Sonia, even dragging him to look at the building in Via Borgelli 11, we devoted only a very minor portion of our time to that sort of topic. An occasional offhand reference, a joke or a wisecrack, and that was all.

We talked about ideas, life, and politics, as is so often the case with young people who, despite everything, secretly hope somehow to leave their mark on the world. A slightly unreal notion in our case, since we lived under a regime that, with a smile, kept a fist firmly clamped around our necks.

Ruben was, like me, a "disapprovant," with the difference

that in our conversations I liked to comment on the situation in which we found ourselves with a sarcastic witticism, while Ruben instead grew heated and built up to a fury. He often grew so angry that his gestures became frantic, and at times he seemed to leap and dance like a clown at the circus.

Perhaps more than for the thefts and misappropriations of the Fascists, to which we had become accustomed, what really drove us into a fury was the attitude of relentless applause of the public at large, that dizzy swirl of popular enthusiasm that greeted every parade, every ridiculous theatrical gesture, that worshipful admiration for Mussolini, portrayed on horseback or else with a crowd of country housewives, dancing in a farmyard.

And so it was in the presence of all this that there began to swell an enormous sense of discouragement and a pressing need to talk to one another about it, as if we two alone were still able to see in the country of the blind.

Yes, of course, I know; there were certainly political activists opposed to the regime, but neither I nor Ruben had any idea where to find them, and perhaps we were not really that interested in trying. But I'm not talking about those who were genuinely involved in a real political struggle. I am talking about the others, those who cheered the Fascists on, while we few managed to glimpse the invisible and insidious web that seemed to be slowly covering our everyday lives, while a faint haze of the ridiculous descended over everything, a ridiculous that gradually turned into something grotesque.

In any case, that particular evening we got together only because I was determined to tell Ruben all about the new and troublesome twist in my love for Sonia.

I remember every detail of that evening distinctly.

Around sunset there had been a downpour with gusting winds. When Ruben and I met, it had stopped raining, but there were still puddles dotting the streets, and on the ground, here and there, piles of drenched leaves as if it were already autumn, and not the beginning of a summer still struggling in its birth throes.

I had watched Ruben come toward me with his distinctive gangling gait, and I was suddenly seized by a very well known sensation, as if I were annoyed and deeply moved at the same time; I sometimes felt it in the presence of excessively familiar images (it happened sometime with my parents as well).

I felt love and impatience: for his figure, not exactly heavyset, but certainly compact, as if something had prevented him from soaring skyward, for the hair that neither aqua nor brilliantine could manage to keep plastered to his head, for his eyes—bewildered and inquisitive—that he seemed to have inherited directly from the patriarch Abraham.

Now we were tramping along side by side, lost in thought as we stepped on the piles of wet leaves. I couldn't bring myself to come to the point, to unburden myself with Ruben about what was foremost in my mind.

And so I started off with the usual topic, politics. Then I had asked Ruben what he thought about the law that had just been issued by the government, requiring all Jews to register as members of one of Italy's Jewish communities. It struck me as yet another abuse of power on the part of the Fascist regime, I told him.

Ruben disagreed with me. The obligation to enroll in a Jewish community, he explained, affected—if you were willing to look at it from a certain, somewhat contrived point of view—only those who wished to be considered Jewish. That said, the law might even prove to be useful in some ways. In fact, it might help to clarify matters within the communities; now they could finally establish clearly who they could rely upon to maintain their own institutions.

"Certain regulations," Ruben concluded somewhat hastily, "may seem a little authoritarian, but in practical terms they may prove to me more functional."

Ruben explained all this to me with a hint of uncertainty in his voice, not because he wasn't really convinced of what he was saying but because he knew as well as I did that the reason we were meeting was certainly not to express our opinions about the Rocco law governing Jewish communities.

At a certain point I understood that I would have to stop digressing, and I talked to Ruben about what had happened.

You may be astonished at how I tell you about my conversation with him, with all the details of what I said to him and how he answered me or didn't answer me, but this is one of the most vivid and burning scenes of my entire life, and not a day goes by without my unreeling it before my mind's eye, caught in time, the way I saw it, because Ruben can no longer reply or modify any part of it.

I started out, more or less as I had with my parents, by telling him and explaining to him with a certain artificial nonchalance the solution of the Pauline marriage.

Ruben listened to me. You have probably figured out what Ruben was like by this point, always ready to leap in with something to say; well, this time he listened and said practically nothing.

A few brief requests for clarifications, much more concise than the questions my father asked, and then he resumed his silence.

You can imagine, therefore, how much greater was my sense of discomfort when I confessed to him (and I could not have done otherwise) the promises that Sonia's father had wormed out of me.

At this point, Ruben stopped talking entirely.

I was shifting from discomfort to a growing irritation. In an agitated tone of voice I urged him to say something to me, anything, for heaven's sake, to accuse me of whatever he wanted, as he had done so often in the past, without worrying about hurting my feelings, I told him to lay into me, but just please stop this intolerable silence.

Since Ruben continued to say nothing, and seemed to be deeply engaged in shifting wet leaves from place to place with one foot, I started to defend myself against accusations that no one had leveled.

I explained to him that I'd done it for Sonia's sake, for all the reasons I've already told you about, as if it were fair somehow to give special consideration to those who really clung to their faith as opposed to those who were largely indifferent, and other things along that line.

I knew, oh how I knew, that this was not the point, and that I was simply muddying the waters in order to keep from having to address the core issue. And in fact, when I finally cried, practically shouting in my exasperation, "Say something!," Ruben replied in a calm and quiet tone.

"It's just a question of self-respect," he said.

It's just a question of self-respect. I couldn't pry another word out of him.

At that point I completely lost my temper. I started shouting, extracting on my own the things that Ruben was *not* saying to me, and then mocking it sarcastically to demonstrate the flimsiness of those nonexistent arguments of his.

"That's fine, I get it, you think I'm like the professor in *The Blue Angel*! Maybe you're just waiting for me to start crowing like a rooster," I blurted bitterly, expecting at least a smirk if not a smile.

Ruben looked at me with a serious expression and said, simply, "Yes." Nothing more. Just "Yes."

There followed a disheartened silence on my part as well.

Sure, I had imagined that Ruben wouldn't be in favor of my decision, and I had already pictured the ensuing scene: a bitter argument, underscored by his frantic leaps and jigs. But I hadn't expected this blank abandonment.

Not only was I losing the heart-to-heart conversation that I needed so badly; the image of Ruben, my enraged interlocutor, was vanishing as well.

From pain I progressed to open revolt. What did Ruben know about passion, Ruben who always fell in love with girls who wound up marrying someone else because they hadn't even noticed that he had feelings for them?

But I didn't say that to him.

I said something else to him, and this time I too was speaking in a low and measured voice.

"Do you want to know the truth? You, who depict yourself as more or less attached to your faith? Well, passion is what brings us closest to God, and it's what persuades even the greatest doubters that God exists."

Now Ruben couldn't help but look at me with a perplexed expression on his face.

"Yes," I was continuing with a growing sense of self-assurance. "When we are all just so many puppets with the ability to reason, then the idea of God in our everyday lives remains an extraneous concern. We grow up, we pursue our studies, we construct careers linked to the things we have studied or trained for, we select a suitable wife. What out of all this remains a mystery? Then, out of the blue, a tempest sweeps down upon us and overturns all our certainties, and we begin to thrash around like madmen. Only then do we begin to understand that in reality we are helpless. We think that we see a clear objective ahead of us, and instead discover that we are stumbling along, no better than a little blind mouse in a labyrinth, And so we find ourselves wandering, storm-tossed like fallen leaves, driven by the winds of life."

By the time I shouted out my last phrase, I was sweaty and waving my arms: "Can't you see that even if you murder someone in the throes of passion, you're still closer to God than if you obediently follow all the rules of the game?"

"Do something! Live! Make mistakes!" I went on shouting. "It's only in the impetus of love and despair that we can hope to find the meaning of the divine in this world!"

I stopped, exhausted. I was ashamed of having indulged myself in this weird rapture. But perhaps more than anything else I had exalted myself with my own words, because then and there I believed that I had come close to hitting the truth.

Ruben kept looking at me the whole time, and the only change that I noticed in his expression was a sweeter, more open look in his eyes, and I didn't know whether that was more a mark of empathy or pity.

Afterwards, he said only one word to me: "Ciao," with an affectionate pat on the shoulder, and he walked slowly away. I saw him in the distance, head down, looking for more piles of wet leaves to kick at gently.

I didn't know if I'd ever see him again.

Later I entered Sonia's house.

That first evening, Sonia dragged me to the window of her bedroom. "Look," she told me, "I have a private moon all my own."

I looked where she was pointing. On the facing roof, there really was a bright patch of light that resembled the round reflection of the full moon.

I looked a little more carefully and saw that it was a kind of porthole in a garret apartment, emanating an opalescent and secret luminosity all its own. But the idea of a private moon became our own treasure from that moment on. And it stayed that way for a long time.

# CHAPTER EIGHT

The first time I entered Sonia's house, it was virtually a product of chance.

This is how it happened. Since we were no longer undercover, one evening when we had tickets for the theater, Sonia intentionally asked me to come up to get her, instead of waiting outside the front door for her to come downstairs.

There was no one at home but the mother and the elderly maid, whom I had already seen in the street.

It struck me that the ancient maid, who can certainly have had no idea that she was flinging open for me the door of life, seemed to glare at me in a fashion that bordered on surly. Maybe it was just an impression, but that she had not given me even the palest hint of a smile was unmistakable.

And that was when Sonia took me by the hand and pulled me at a run down the hallway to her bedroom. There, she showed me the view from her window of her own private moon, the mysterious dormer window where, in the summer twilight, someone had already switched on a pale opalescent light.

I hadn't even glanced at the rest of the apartment, but you should keep in mind that I was rushed and bewildered, and at first I hadn't grasped the reason that we were running hand in hand down the hallway.

When we returned to the front hall, ready to leave the house for the theater, her mother appeared—Signora Adelaide, whom I had met at the private clinic.

She extended her hand in my direction; she, for one, stretched her lips into a smile, and then in a fairly neutral voice she informed me that every Saturday evening the family dined at home, including Renato Martini, Clotilde's fiancé, and that therefore . . . in other words, and here Sonia's mother seemed on the verge of unhappily opening her jaws wide for the tools of an unseen dentist . . . from now on, I would also be a welcome dinner guest.

When we walked out of the house, Sonia was beside herself with joy, though I couldn't quite tell whether it was out of the excitement of having finally shared with me a glimpse of her private moon or simply because of that official invitation extended by her mother.

In any case, Sonia had already become bubbly and exuberant in a way that I had never seen before. Of course, I had always sensed the intensity of her feelings for me, followed later by that wave of compressed pain, which became practically intolerable when it seemed at first that we would never be able to construct a life together.

Now, though, alongside the love there was a filigree of childish happiness, an exaggerated enthusiasm for everything we did together, so that even an evening out at the theater for a show became *the* evening out at *the* theater for *the* show of shows of *all* the theaters on earth.

That Sonia could never find happiness with me unless she had the framework of her parents and her sisters to surround us, in other words, without the seal of approval of her family, had been clear to me almost from the beginning. Sonia was an inseparable part of Via Borgelli 11, with the bougainvillea climbing up the façade and the dormer window atop the building across the way, disguised as a private moon. But now there was something more.

Sonia was grateful to me. She had sensed the strain of the many compromises that I had laboriously negotiated with myself in order to make my way to her, and I could sense her gratitude in every gesture, in every word, as if I were the prince in the fairy tale who had given up his throne to prove his love.

Little by little, I had told her about my conversation with Ruben, and it saddened Sonia greatly.

"But why?" she asked me from time to time in anguish, as if deep down she subconsciously understood what Ruben meant to say, but Ruben represented to her nothing more than a small corner of unhappiness that had unexpectedly come to spoil our beautiful celebration of love.

She'd ask me: "Why?" and I'd answer her, "That's just the way Ruben is," a phrase that meant nothing and explained nothing. But I wasn't comfortable letting Sonia venture into the deeper territories of Ruben. It would have meant betraying him a second time, if betrayal was the right word to describe what had happened between him and me.

Then Sonia would throw her arms around me and say, "I'm sorry, I'm so sorry, it's all my fault," and then she would exclaim in a sort of rapture, "I'll make it up to you, you'll always be happy with me."

To reassure her, I told her about my parents and that, after all, they hadn't seemed to be very upset.

"I want to go back to the Albergo della Magnolia," Sonia would say, contented and cheerful once again, "but this time I want to see your magnolia tree, not the floor of the ballroom."

On 20 June 1930 I made my official entrance into the house at Via Borgelli 11. The apartment, up on the top floor, stretched out lazily, gobbling up all the floor space that on all the other landings was divided up between two or three apartments.

Once again, the stern-faced housekeeper let me in; this time she was wearing a black apron that was shinier than usual, a sort of gala uniform.

I have a few sketchy memories of my first impressions: the vast living room with an assortment of round, well-upholstered

easy chairs that immediately made me think of so many dough-
nuts ready for a giant's breakfast, a succession of soft and identical carpets, then a set of antique, intricately hand-carved
chairs that must have been fantastically uncomfortable to sit in,
and, last of all, the French doors, with their dark woodwork and
panels of glass, which, once opened, led to the dining room.

I was stunned to see the entire family together. There was
Signora Adelaide with her usual gaze of feigned short-sighted-
ness, Dottore Giuseppe Gentile who shook my hand with the
sort of condescending cordiality one uses with underlings, the
pretty Clotilde, staring haughtily into the middle distance as
usual, and Renato Martini, her fiancé, tall, elegant, a perfect
match for her, with the addition of a mustachio.

As Martini reached out to shake hands with me, he said, "It's
a pleasure," as if he hadn't already met me. I've never understood whether he had actually forgotten the events of New
Year's Eve or whether he considered it indelicate to refer to
them, as if we had chanced to meet in, just for the sake of an
example, a brothel or some other unseemly location.

Only one family member was absent: Lorenza, who arrived
late and slightly disheveled, drawing a murmured reproof from
her mother.

I was sitting in one of the doughnut-chairs and forcing
myself to sip from a glass of sickly sweet vermouth, trying to
think of something to say, when the housekeeper entered the
room and whispered a few words almost directly into the prof-
fered ear of the lady of the house.

Signora Adelaide leapt to her feet. "I believe it's ready," she
announced in a loud and joyful voice, adorning, for some
unknown reason, with an ornamental "I believe" the information that she had just been given about the meal. "To the dining
room, everyone!" she added more explicitly, accompanying the
second phrase with a quick clap of her hands.

And so we all moved through the French doors.

The table gleamed with decorated dishes, engraved crystal drinking glasses, and silver place settings, arranged in a rigid, almost maniacal order, one utensil alongside another.

"There, every place is taken. Now if I get engaged too, what are we supposed to do?" Lorenza grumbled audibly, and her mother shot her a smoldering retort—"Don't be ridiculous, you're only fifteen"—while her brother-in-law-to-be Renato Martini looked at her and snickered.

The first period of dinner-table conversation, I have to admit, struck me as phenomenally dull. Everyone was talking about people I had never met and describing situations and events of no interest whatsoever, routine occurrences of distressing banality. In connection with certain of the individuals mentioned, there were accounts of developments that no one, even in the most indulgent state of mind, could possibly have flattered with the title of "anecdotes."

I can't say how or why, but as I sat there at the dinner table, there suddenly popped into my mind the image of one of the family dinners at the house of my Aunt Esterina.

I had never been especially enthusiastic about big family dinners; in fact, I always did my best to avoid them whenever possible. And so I have to guess that the vision of a dinner at Aunt Esterina's that popped into my mind of its own accord was probably an act of spite on the part of my rebellious subconscious.

There I sat, like a boarding-school student who felt a moral obligation to construct a sense of homesickness; there I sat imagining myself back at Aunt Esterina's dinner table. The first thing I thought was that at Aunt Esterina's house an outsider might feel uncomfortable, obliged to listen to stories about people he had never met. Immediately following that thought, however, came the distinct sensation that a dinner there would have been quite different as experienced by an outsider. And I reviewed in my mind's eye all those scenes of intertwining conversations, people interrupting one another, just to clarify, explain, and impose one's own point of view.

No one eating dinner at Aunt Esterina's house would ever need to ask "Who are you talking about?" Every character who appeared in a conversation had certainly already been abundantly introduced, presented, described, and discussed in every aspect of his or her appearance and personality during those long dinners.

What did these comparisons of extended families have to do with my present situation, especially in connection with events that never meant much of anything to me? And now of all times, during the happiest evening of my life, the evening in which I was officially admitted into the inner circle of Sonia's family?

As I told you before, I have no other explanation except for the hypothesis of an attempted sabotage by my increasingly quarrelsome subconscious.

But I want to proceed with an account of that memorable evening, the night of my first dinner in Sonia's home. I have often played a game with myself of remembering every slightest detail, and I certainly don't want to miss this opportunity to put them all down on paper.

And so. Dinner was proceeding. Out of nowhere another, younger housekeeper had appeared, with a plump ruddy country face. When she approached me with the serving dish, I thought for a moment that I felt a slight pressure on my elbow. I looked up in astonishment, and I saw that she was using her eyes to point me to the slice of meat she wanted me to take, unquestionably the best cut on the dish.

Suddenly it struck me that no one at that table, with the obvious exception of Sonia, had any particular liking for me. But now, that little country housekeeper . . .

I have to say that I was wrong, though. Yes, with the passing of time I understood how wrong I had been. For instance, I was wrong about Lorenza. Lorenza was standoffish and combative, but her hostility was certainly not directed at me in particular, quite the contrary.

And I was wrong about the young maid, who had certainly not been swept away by any sudden attraction to me. It was something quite different. What she felt toward me was, so to speak, a form of class solidarity. She saw me, more or less, as a peer: an outsider, a stray dog whom she was trying to protect in that world of the wealthy. And the same motive, though in reverse, was what drove the surly hostility of the head housekeeper, who was wholly aligned with the spirit of the house.

As dinner proceeded, the conversation shifted to the game of bridge.

"If you could have seen the expression on your face when you heard that Clotilde plays bridge too!" Sonia said to me later, laughing, when we were finally alone. "You think she's too stupid even to play a game, if it demands even a little bit of thinking, don't you?"

I didn't answer her question, but my expression must have been pretty eloquent. In response, Sonia set forth a theory of hers, a theory of—shall we say—"sectorial intelligence," an aspect of mental circulation whereby all of a person's abilities are concentrated on a single point.

This theory made quite an impression upon me, because I was reminded of it in other circumstances of my life. There are people who are brilliant in one specific area and completely useless in every other walk of life.

Before drawing the curtain on that evening, and I hope you'll forgive me if it's becoming tedious (though that is how it "rang through the darkness of my heart"), I should at least describe the only moment in which I finally had a role to play.

At that point we were talking about horses, because horses, I learned, were the second love of Clotilde's fiancé's life. Renato, everyone knew, was a first-rate horseman, and he had taken awards more than once in the national competitions of the GUF, the Fascist student association.

For the first time, unexpectedly, Renato turned toward me and asked me point-blank if I liked horses.

I told him that I admired horses greatly from an aesthetic point of view, especially in the enchanting depictions and images of horses and riders that I had encountered in my readings of the Greek poets.

It was a clumsy and contrived answer, typical of a classics professor, you might well say, but otherwise I couldn't have thought of a thing to say. And so I quoted Pindar's "tireless-footed horses," an expression that my favorite poet used frequently and that I had always liked.

There was a moment of silence, and then Clotilde spoke up. "Tireless-footed horses," she repeated, musingly, and added that it really was a sweet expression. Then she asked me if Pindar had written other things of this sort.

I was nonplused at first, but then I recovered my wits and I mentioned Heléna (Helen, the seductress from the Trojan War), whom Pindar invariably described as "a curly-haired beauty."

Once again, Clotilde fell silent in thought. I took advantage of the lull to explain the lovely and concise power of the expression. When I was done, Clotilde appeared to be convinced, smiled at me, and said that, in fact, Pindar really must be very sweet.

And so, with "sweet Pindar" (You see? Pindar had proved useful after all), I had finally found a space for myself in that evening's dinner.

# CHAPTER NINE

I n Sonia's family, as you may have already understood, Fascism was part and parcel with the doughnut-shaped easy chairs and the eighty-four-piece set of crystal.

That we should all enthusiastically support the Duce was such an obvious conclusion that it seemed inconceivable to the entire family that anyone might see things differently.

Once, at the dinner table, Signora Adelaide turned to me with great excitement (from time to time she emerged from her state of detachment) and said: "How do you explain, Professor, the charisma of Mussolini?"

I answered cautiously that, yes, in fact, Mussolini seemed to appeal to women, and while I struggled to produce a generic explanation for his allure, Sonia's mother interrupted and, with a coquettish air that she believed, mistakenly, suited her particularly well, she said: "Not only to women, from what I hear, Professor . . ." And so it went. I uttered an incomplete and entirely half-baked sentence, and before I knew it I had been enrolled in the vast army of those who were enamored of Mussolini.

For that matter, the other son-in-law, Renato Martini, even though he had finished his studies at the university some time ago, was still an executive officer of the GUF, and he used his position as a base for his political activism.

Sonia and I had talked about it. I had explained to her my views on Fascism one of the very first times we had an opportunity to talk together for hours and hours. She had listened to me, at first in astonishment, then with growing interest and a deepening awareness, focused intently on what I was telling her.

When I met Sonia, she was twenty years old, and so she had grown up while Fascism grew alongside her. No one had ever pointed out to her that not everything was going perfectly under the regime.

She had even considered the murder of Giacomo Matteotti, it seemed to me, based on the scanty information she had picked up from those around her, as nothing more than one of those regrettable political intrigues that occur practically everywhere, in every age and under every government.

I began from that very same event—from Matteotti—and led her through a sort of historical review of our recent national past, motivated, of course, by a desire to convince her, to persuade her to agree with my own ideas, but also driven by that love of instruction that is an intrinsic trait of every male ever born, and therefore all the more marked in someone who was, like me, a professor.

And so, secretly, deep down I melded together a legitimate aspiration to open Sonia's eyes to the way things really stood in our country and a desire to make her my student, though of course, I only see that now, many years later.

In any case, I must have been a good teacher, because Sonia very quickly became an alert and convinced "disapprovant," just like me.

Certainly, it wasn't like when I had a good argument with Ruben. I missed Ruben. I missed his furious rages and his little hop, skip, and jump of indignation. With Sonia I felt only comforted, supported. But that was already something.

Just a few days earlier, the principal of my school, old Professor Palmieri, to whom I was very attached, had been replaced. He had been forced out of his job because of the provision in the new law issued by the Grand Council that required university chancellors and school principals to be chosen from among the faculty members who had at least five years' seniority as registered members of the National Fascist Party. And Palmieri couldn't claim that seniority.

Now, in place of my old friend, the principal of the school was a pompous individual whose interest in culture was the furthest thing from his mind. Encounters with this sort of person, I can assure you, were anything but agreeable.

I told Sonia about these things, and I sensed that she shared my disappointment, the sense of frustration that overwhelmed me to the verge of paralysis. As I mentioned, her subdued support had become very important to me.

Of course, our conversations remained between us. Sonia, despite her love for her family, would never have dreamed of talking with them about any of the things she and I discussed.

By now, I had a better understanding of which subjects could be brought up at our Saturday dinners and which couldn't, and all things considered, I'd become a little more sophisticated in my behavior. Now I was receiving the occasional spontaneous invitation to other entertainments and meals, and the only real difference was in the uniform worn on those occasions by the housekeepers: it was a little less formal. Also, the drinking glasses weren't made of cut crystal and the array of utensils was slightly less imposing.

One day, I was informed that the Gentile family intended to hold an official reception for my parents. The general attitude struck me as similar to the first time that Signora Adelaide invited me to dinner, her mouth gaping in resignation, awaiting the dentist's tools; the prevailing atmosphere was that of something that can't be avoided.

I won't bore you with another description of the details of yet another dinner; at this point I've already described everything, and of course, given the occasion, every detail was at its finest.

No one will ever disabuse me of the notion that deep down,

the Gentile family hoped with all this magnificent pomp and circumstance to intimidate their guests, and they assumed that my parents belonged to a category that they looked down upon, in terms of personal wealth and social standing.

They were mistaken.

They were mistaken in the sense that they had overlooked certain factors. My parents were hoteliers, and they had long ago become accustomed, indeed inured, to imposing ranks of silverware, silver chargers, and other exquisite place settings; they barely noticed such things.

As for the conversation: after all, my father was a businessman himself, and he was accustomed to doing business on an international stage; among other things, he spoke three foreign languages fluently.

Dottore Gentile, without even meaning to, and perhaps without realizing that he was doing so, found himself asking question after question, and then listening attentively and with unmistakable interest. Finally Giuseppe Gentile had insisted on asking my father what his foreign clientele thought about what was happening in Italy, and especially whether they admired what this new Italy was achieving.

My father didn't even have to lie. In fact, nearly all his foreign customers were great admirers of Mussolini's Italy.

At a certain point, my mother was a little more reckless. Given an opening by a glancing question about the Albergo della Magnolia, she spread her wings and took to the conversational skies, swooping and capering happily through the kingdom of her delight. She plunged in, surfaced, and dove back down into the deep blue domain of the hotel, recounting arcane details of its inner workings, unveiling them with the cautious circumspection that one would use when handling authentic national secrets. She concluded with a meticulous account of the renovation of the furnishings, which she had planned and executed in collaboration with the interior designer, yes, none other than the mastermind of the fatal raised dance floor.

Signora Adelaide looked at her somewhat taken aback, but I have to confess that my mother, with her running patter, like that of an overexuberant schoolgirl, was quite likable, and she had prevented—albeit a little too passionately—the conversation from languishing.

After dinner there was a solemn and slightly ridiculous moment—in other words, we all found ourselves in the midst of an occasion straight out of a nineteenth-century novel.

Dottore Gentile had summoned my father into his study.

The following day my father, with the awkward embarrassment that came to him whenever he had to talk about private matters, told me what Sonia's father had imparted to him. In short, when Sonia was married, he would endow the happy couple with an apartment, and the budding family, thanks to the lump sum that would be given as a dowry, could rely on a supplementary stream of income. The same conditions applied to the other daughters, he noted hastily.

I had more or less been informed of these gifts by Sonia, but my father's uneasiness proved contagious. I felt very uncomfortable for the first time, as if by accepting these facilitations in life from the Gentile family, I was somehow betraying both my father and myself, even more than when I had agreed to the request concerning religion. Adding to this discomfort was the fact that my father rarely talked to me about what he considered to be my own business.

"You will become a university professor," my father then murmured with even greater effort, and it was unclear to me whether he was asking a question or simply stating a fact of which he had been informed by chance.

And in fact, as Giuseppe Gentile introduced me to friends and acquaintances, he described me confidently as "a future star of our university system," which unfailingly met with a ceremonious and knowing congratulation from one and all—an ostentatious and ceremonial delight.

In concrete terms, Sonia's father had put me in touch with the editors of a number of prestigious journals of Hellenic studies, and I had begun to contribute, sending them essays and studies on various topics.

Actually, my essay entitled "Archilocus, a François Villon of the Classical World" had enjoyed a certain success (among other scholars, of course), but to assume on that basis that I was already on the path to a university chair, well, I still had a long way to go, at least according to the way I saw things. But perhaps Giuseppe Gentile saw things differently from me.

"The university is still a pretty distant goal for now," I had told my father. "I still need to take the qualifying exam to teach high school." I may have misinterpreted, but for some reason it struck me that my father was relieved.

The summer sun was already beating down fiercely hot. It promised to be a beautiful summer.

School was over for the year and activities of every sort were lazily winding down in the heat and with a view to the approaching summer holidays. My parents had made an attempt to return the courtesy, by extending an invitation to the Gentile family for dinner, but of course our dining room was nothing more than a secluded corner of the dining room of the Albergo della Magnolia, cordoned off by potted plants.

The Gentile family seemed somewhat nonplussed. After all, the invitation from the groom's parents is meant to familiarize the bride's family with the groom's home, so why would the invitation be to have dinner in a hotel dining room?

Well, the response came back, it was late in the season, let's talk about it in the autumn. And when autumn came, it brought no dinner with it. In October, the main preoccupation was with Clotilde's wedding; there was no time to worry about having a hotel restaurant dinner with the Carpi family.

\*

One day, recovering her society matron's tone of voice, Signora Adelaide urged me, "Professor, make sure you're free next Tuesday; our cousin Gherardo will be in town, and he has assured us that his first stop will be at our house. I absolutely want you to meet him."

"Oh, good!" said Clotilde, who for the occasion had managed to insert a little expression into her voice. "Cousin Gherardo is coming, I'm so pleased!" This Cousin Gherardo must be quite some personality if he could move Clotilde out of her habitual state of ataraxy.

Gherardo was technically the first cousin of the master of the house, since their respective fathers had been siblings, but there was a considerable difference in age. But this very difference in age—Gherardo had not yet turned forty—meant that Gherardo, who had no family ties apart from his mother, was more comfortable hanging around with the daughters. In a sense, he was a cousin on loan to the younger generation.

While they were talking about him, they recounted a wealth of other details. That Gherardo lived in Tuscany where his mother (and therefore where Gherardo as well) owned an immense vineyard; that his mother was the Contessa Colonnesi, an iron lady, though a somewhat eccentric one; that together they owned the venerable castle of Murmuzio (tenth century, Signora Adelaide informed us in a punctilious aside), but that for the past two generations, the family no longer chose to reside in the castle, preferring instead a cozy and comfortable villa ("*bellissima, bellissima*" cried Clotilde, perking up), and that Gherardo lived part of the time there, part of the time in an apartment he owned in Florence, and was frequently on the road, crisscrossing Italy, on the circuit of art exhibitions, festival, and other events of that sort . . .

"He's not married, as far as I can tell," I noted.

"Ah, *sì*, that one's engaged to be married with that mother of his," Lorenza blurted out, in a fairly unsuccessful imitation of a Tuscan accent.

"Don't talk nonsense, you impossibly rude child!" Signora Adelaide slapped her down, truly angry this time. The very idea! She was singing the praises of such well-born people and that ill-mannered daughter of hers had to butt in and ruin everything, as usual . . .

Sonia smiled at me, as if to say "Don't listen to her," but it was clear that she was amused.

And that's how it went. This was the first time that I heard anyone mention Cousin Gherardo, the last character of the play, the last one needed to fill out the cast of our story.

Then Gherardo and I met.

# Chapter Ten

Gherardo? Gherardo, by the time I arrived at the house in the Via Borgelli, must have been there for a good long while. It was evident from his relaxed posture, reclining comfortably on the sofa in the living room, as well as from the way that all three girls looked up at me with a slightly dazed expression when I walked into the room, as if my appearance was calculated to break in on their enjoyable chitchat. Yes, even Sonia had glanced up at me with a distracted air—though only for an instant, and she had recovered her normal attitude immediately.

Gherardo when I first met him: he was dressed in white linen, I remember that clearly, and I also remember thinking to myself, "No, you couldn't call him elegant." He made a strange and immediate impression on me, a sprawling, chaotic figure, invariably at odds with his surroundings, a head of hair that defied all attempts to tame it, tossing wildly without restraint in any direction it chose at that moment.

The more I looked at him, the longer I listened to him speak, the more a kind of astonishment welled up in me, because Gherardo, uniquely, managed to reconcile within himself a quality of absolute imperturbability and a despairing restlessness.

He looked sharply over at me for a fleeting instant, then let his gaze shift immediately away to wander elsewhere.

"Dino, isn't it?" he spoke to me a second later in a neutral tone of voice, fixing me again with a curious glance. "I already know all about you. I got here early just so they could tell me everything."

"I can always provide a quick refresher course," I ventured, but the quip fell flat. Just then the other two men of the family were entering the room: the master of the house and Clotilde's fiancé, while Signora Adelaide, after a quick confab with the housekeeper, stood ready to recite her line: "I believe it's ready."

As we all rose and began moving toward the French doors I happened to glance over at the figures of the two young men attending that evening (aside from me, of course), Renato Martini and Gherardo, both tall and slender. Renato Martini, however, was impeccable in his manner, like an officer of the Savoy Cavalry Regiment, while Gerardo was elongated, as flimsy as a tree branch that is longer than it is sturdy.

Once we were seated, Gherardo, at his cousin's insistence, began to supply a few reluctant details about his new Isotta-Fraschini. Some of his answers seemed to be chosen at random; he clearly had not listened to the question at all. He then excused himself, claiming to be simply exhausted.

"What kind of work do you do?" I asked in an attempt to change the subject, since Gherardo had made it perfectly clear, almost ostentatiously clear, that he didn't enjoy talking about cars.

"What kind of work do I do? I wouldn't dream of being so selfish, with the economy in its current state, as to take employment from an honest laborer!"

"What a sterling paragon of selfless devotion," I murmured under my breath, and Gherardo swung around, wide-eyed.

"I cannot believe my ears—sitting at this table for once is a human being capable of uttering a witticism!" Gherardo had come to life again, and from that moment on—apparently forgetful of his proclaimed exhaustion—he never left my side. For the rest of the evening, I realized very soon, every word he uttered was directed to me and no one other than me.

"To tell the truth, I don't work because I don't need any-thing," he corrected himself slyly. "I have the simplest tastes. I am always satisfied with the best."

"I see we have a friend in common," I promptly shot back. I had recognized the reference and I knew the author he was quoting. I wanted to let him know, but he had clearly taken that for granted.

"Well, I do try to lend a hand on the estate," he added, addressing the table. "Though of course my mother is happier when I don't bother."

Then he explained in a neutral tone of voice that actually from time to time he did help his mother to supervise the estate, but that he really couldn't be sure his mother was happy for him to help, in fact he sometimes thought she preferred for him not to. "That's why she insisted on buying me the Isotta-Fraschini, so that I'd be gone more frequently," he added with conviction.

At this point, Signora Adelaide felt called upon to intervene. She contradicted him vigorously, stating emphatically that the Contessa wouldn't be able to manage without his help.

"Sure . . ." Gherardo seemed to be lost in thought for a moment, but then, with one of his sudden starts, he turned to me and said: "I'll bet they told you that my mother and I are like a pair of lovers."

At this point, while Signora Adelaide seemed momentarily unable to breathe, I saw Lorenza—and this was the first and only time I saw anything of the sort—turn bright pink. Lorenza, always sure of herself and impudent, was staring at me with a look of disquiet and reproof, as if I (but when could I have done it?) had reported to her cousin the words she had spoken a few days before.

"I know perfectly well that's what people say about us," Gherardo continued, undaunted. "You know, my mother's per-sonality isn't something I'd wish on anyone else, but her intelligence . . . I confess, she has a wit and insight I've never seen in any other woman. She reads every book that comes out, she knows all the gossip of the theater world, the movies, art, and culture in general . . . How can she do it? She converses with everyone, she matches wits with everyone. She entertained D'Annunzio as a guest at our house. It seems understandable, I think, that someone would find her company amusing . . . even if that person is her son, don't you agree? But after a while it's my mother who gets tired of me—she says that she needs a little space."

"And that's fine." Lorenza had recovered and it was evident that she intended to wade bravely into what she considered to have been her own gaffe thoughtlessly reported to her cousin. "Your mother may well be just as you describe her, but that hardly seems like sufficient reason for you not to be able to find a girlfriend, a fiancée . . ."

"Lorenza! What business is that of yours?" Signora Adelaide had just recovered and her relentlessly inappropriate daughter was back at work spreading havoc.

"No, no, let her talk, she has a point. She has a point, but she has her facts wrong. I was engaged to be married once, engaged for almost three days, I'll admit, but I did have a fiancée. It was the most nightmarish experience of my life. One morning I woke up and found myself thinking, 'Tonight we're going to the theater.' *We're going*, you see, not 'Tonight I'm going.' I realized that I would never be able to conjugate in the first-person singular any of a number of verbs: I'll go, or I'm doing, I'm leaving, I return . . . Isn't that the most chilling thought that a person can have? I mean, that strikes me as hell, hell on earth and hell in eternity . . ."

Clotilde at this point unexpectedly spoke up, saying that it was merely a matter of finding the right person.

"Well sure, I imagine you're right, that must be the case. You just need to find the right person. Easier said than done, though! We live in a vulgar age, everything inevitably smacks of such bad taste!"

"Now don't exaggerate; quite frankly, I fail to see all this bad taste you describe, at least not in the past few years," the master of the house felt obliged to insist. "Great Caesar's ghost, you're going a bit too far . . ."

I remember very clearly that after these words Gherardo began to declaim.

"Get hold of a good photograph of Signor Mussolini some time and study it," he was saying, in the tone of someone adressing a crowd. "You will see the weakness in his mouth which forces him to scowl the famous Mussolini scowl. And then look at his black shirt and his white spats. There is something wrong, even histrionically, with a man who wears white spats with a black shirt."

"Gherardo, I will not tolerate this from you!" Such was Giuseppe Gentile's indignation that he had actually risen to his feet. Then he mastered his emotions; he chose not to attribute excessive importance to the matter. "You're not at all amusing with these egg-headed lucubrations . . . You shouldn't spout such stuff, not even within these walls, and one day or another . . ."

"Those words aren't Gherardo's; Ernest Hemingway wrote that in 1922, eight years ago." My tone of voice was intended to convey a justification of what Gherardo was saying, but deep down, I really meant to subtly reinforce his point, by attributing them to their true, far more illustrious author.

"It's true, I'm quoting Hemingway, but when I first read those words they made a big impression on me, and I never forgot them." Gherardo was smiling at me, winking as if to say, "I never seem to be able to pull the wool over your eyes, you sly dog."

"Well, in any case, it's dangerous to play around with ideas like that, even at home." Giuseppe Gentile, still somewhat indignant, cast a quick glance around the room, beginning with the furrowed brow of Renato Martini and winding up on the far wall.

Was the housekeeper (by the way, the older one was named Anatolia and the younger one was named Pasqua) present for the tirade? Had she heard? Just now, there was no one in the room, but before, who could say?

" 'An idea that is not dangerous is unworthy of being called an idea at all' . . . It's Wilde again," Gherardo beat me to the punch with a laugh. "Don't get upset," he said, turning to his cousin. "I may joke around, but I have my feet firmly on the ground. We gave loads of money to the Fascist Party when there were riots in the countryside, and the *Podestà* comes to our house for dinner at least once a week . . . My dear cousins, we are all perfect Fascists, aren't we?" and Gherardo shot yet another glance in my direction.

I said nothing; I kept my face motionless, not allowing even a muscle to twitch. The way that Gherardo was playing cat-and-mouse was beginning to irritate me.

Gherardo sensed the tension in the air and so he began talking again, this time avoiding controversial issues—he talked about his new car, he described the trip he had taken to Venice to see the new Futurist exhibition, and he made a big point of expressing in colorful terms his admiration for the paintings of Balla.

He talked and talked, peppering his conversation with jokes and good cheer, and he was soon amusing everyone in the dining room. There were no more outbursts or protests.

When it was time to leave, he utterly ignored Renato Martini and offered to drive me home in his new car. I told him that I was just a short distance away, that my hotel was in the same neighborhood, and that I was accustomed to walking home.

"Your hotel! What a fine idea! I would like to live in a hotel myself; I like staying in a hotel when I come to Rome. It was really a mistake to buy a place in Florence . . . I just did it because I love to buy paintings and I wouldn't know where to hang them otherwise."

Sonia patiently tried to explain in just a few words that I was not a guest at the Albergo della Magnolia but, rather, the owner, and Gherardo slapped his forehead with one hand. "The hotel-keeper!" he cried, pointing at me with the index finger of the other hand. "Of course, now I remember. Adelaide wrote that tragic letter to my mother all those many months ago." And while Sonia's mother appeared dangerously close to toppling over in a dead faint, her face rapidly passing through an astonishing spectrum of hues, he said, "Just think, Dino, when I heard about it I imagined you as a tavernkeeper with a checkered apron!" And Gherardo, laughing amidst a general wave of consternation, seized me by the arm and was hurrying me downstairs, where he practically heaved me into the passenger seat of his Isotta-Fraschini.

What we said to one another while driving in that car and over the course of a long night I'll tell you in just a moment.

Perhaps it was there that I first began to unravel one of the knots of understanding who I was and what I was doing, but I would only become aware of that many, many years later.

# CHAPTER ELEVEN

A s soon as we climbed into the car, Gherardo appeared a changed man. Laconic and grim-faced, he launched the car jerkily into gear and then sped off, driving at a frenzied pace, without the courtesy of informing me where we were headed, nor asking if there was someplace he could drop me off along the way.

He accelerated wildly as he drove and drove through the Roman night, in the summer heat, dropping down from the heights of our neighborhood to the river, turning at speed onto the deserted road running along the banks of the Tiber and then climbing again—this time I guessed the destination—toward the Janiculum.

He was so grim, remote, and inert. I was not about to be the one to break the tense silence. I was beginning to come to the conclusion that Gherardo always needed an audience to show off his excited and brilliant conversation, and that if he had no audience he simply plunged into a sort of paralysis, unable to think of anything to say.

But that's not the way it was. Once we pulled up to the Piazzale del Gianicolo, with all of Rome glittering at our feet and the starry sky overhead, Gherardo slammed on the brakes so suddenly that as the car screeched to a halt, I found myself jerked forward until my forehead hit the windshield in front of me.

"What are you doing in the midst of that family!" he shouted at me, pounding the steering wheel with both fists.

To say that I was speechless is an understatement: in part I was astonished at his sudden shift into the informal "tu," something that is nowadays all too common (in the country where I now live all we have is the informal), but back then, in the Italy of 1930, to shift unexpectedly into the "tu" form, and moreover in a vigorous shout, was a major factor in rendering me both breathless and speechless.

Yes, you might well say that I focused on the "tu" and not on the essence of the phrase, in an instinctive attempt to avoid the gist of the problem. Still, it's true. I remember that even before I made any attempt to understand what the devil Gherardo was saying to me, I found myself caught up with that aggravating detail, in part because it had so suddenly interrupted at least a quarter of an hour of tense and absolute silence.

"Anyone, anyone with half a brain, would run for their lives to get away from a family like that," Gherardo went on shouting. "But not you! Oh, no. You try to become part of it. You want to become a member of that family at any cost!"

"B-but . . ." I stammered. I was still astonished at his outburst, and I was frantically trying to overcome my amazement and think of some reasonable objection to his tirade.

"Yes, I know, I know. You want to marry Sonia. But the rest of them? Who asked you to marry the whole family?"

Gherardo went on asking questions and answering them without waiting for me.

"Sonia is very close to her family," I finally managed to say, though I had not entirely recovered from that unexpected and vehement attack.

"Of course, the pearl and the oyster . . . you have to take one with the other. Sonia was born that way, I know her too, and I may even have met her a few years before you did."

"So . . . since you know her . . . I don't understand what you're saying to me and why you're getting so angry about it."

My tone of voice was finally rising and regaining a bit of self-confidence. "I made a difficult choice, but the reason strikes me as self-evident: you put it very well, the pearl and the oyster together. I couldn't change Sonia's basic nature in order to make her mine."

"Why am I so angry?" Gherardo continued to follow his own line of reasoning, without a sign of having heard anything I had said. "I'm angry because I can't stand the idea that in this society we live in, where you need the lantern of Diogenes to find one of those all-too-rare individuals who have even a smidgeon of awareness, cultivation, sense of humor, and whatever else you care to throw into the mix—and so, when you finally meet one, you have to watch as he tries to please a group of people who couldn't care less about these things, people that he should scorn. And that's why I'm angry. I consider it a personal matter, a question of taste—a question of good taste."

"I'm not a personal matter of yours!" I shot back angrily. "In fact, I'm none of your business at all!"

"I don't know about that. In fact, I'd say you were. Have you taken a good look at that family? Not a word that is spoken at their dinner table is worth the breath expended in saying it. Much less the trouble of listening. They're handsome, well-dressed people, with plenty of money, but I can't imagine why that would interest you."

"What interests me is Sonia. Evidently, you've never been in love, you can't understand or even guess just what—just what Sonia really is . . ."

"You're wrong there, I understand, I assure you. Sonia isn't stupid like her mother and her sister Clotilde. Sonia is . . . is harmonious . . . that girl somehow manages to make sense of the timeless flows of nature in their finest aspect . . ."

Now Gherardo seemed to be lost in the image of that woman and his voice had turned vague and dreamy; then he recovered. "Sonia is a hothouse flower, but without the glass protection of her hothouse, who can say . . ."

Despite my resentment for Gherardo, I have to admit that I was struck by the words he had said about Sonia and by the fact that he had described her as "harmonious." You know that "harmonious" was the word I had used to describe Sonia from the very beginning. I sensed that Gherardo allowed himself to be swept away by waves of intuition that appeared to surge at sudden intervals from unfathomable depths, but that this always seemed to sweep him up onto a precise and accurate stretch of beach.

"I prefer Lorenza," Gherardo went on, unruffled, suddenly dropping the topic of Sonia. "She may not be as pretty as her sisters, but that's actually her best point. Lorenza has a personal quality, something independent about her. I think that before long she'll wind up leaving that family."

"Listen." My sense of surprise and also of having been offended was slowly subsiding. I felt calmer now; in fact, I felt an urgent need to clarify matters. "I don't understand why you're so angry at me," I said slowly. "If I wanted Sonia I had to accept her family, and that strikes me as perfectly normal. And you can see Sonia's nature, the way she's all bound up with the shell she was born from, so why this sudden astonishment of yours?"

"Don't try to blur the lines! Don't you patronize my intelligence!" I felt calm now, but Gherardo clearly did not, and he went talking to me in a tense, almost angry tone of voice. "We agree on this point. You did anything you could to win Sonia, you agreed to certain compromises in order to gain the family's consent. Everything up to here is clear. But that should have been all. Once you had obtained the fatal 'yes' you could easily, so to speak, 'disappear.' Relations between you and them should have been reduced to courtesy, good manners, hellos and good-byes, smiles, tipping your hat, and nothing more, only the occasional social encounter. But that's not how it went."

"What are you saying?!" I murmured in renewed shock. "That's exactly how it had to be."

"No, it's not! *You want that family to like you.* And not for Sonia's sake, for yourself. You not only want them to accept you as a future husband, no, you want them to like you for yourself, I'll say it again. Practically more than anything else, what you want is for these people, who are less educated than you, less intelligent and less perceptive than you, people with personal values straight out of the Sunday supplement, the *Domenica del Corriere*, to open their arms; you want them to respect you, admire you, consider you one of their own. In fact, it's entirely the reverse, their hidden contempt is not even all that well hidden. You are nothing to people like them, or maybe less than nothing because they are annoyed at the very sight of you. And that's why I get so angry, now do you begin to understand?"

"What could you possibly know about me? You met me this evening for the very first time."

"I may have known you only over the course of a single evening, but it wasn't just the two of us talking over dinner. The general conversation had its ritual phases, the usual, obvious ones, and I paid very close attention to them. Also, I believe that I am sufficiently skilled at teasing information out of other people to be able to pick up all that is needed. You can deny it for the rest of your life, but I am certain that what I've said to you is the absolute truth. That is why I was determined to talk to you about it, to warn you of the dangers, to help you to understand."

"You accuse me of adulation, and that's a serious charge. Why on earth should I act that way?" Now I sensed once again that I was expressing myself poorly, awkwardly. Maybe he really had caught me red-handed, maybe he had struck a fatal blow, but I was still doing my best to react. "Why should I? Explain it to me. If not for Sonia, what the hell reason would I have to do that?"

"How should I know? You're a Jew, aren't you? Maybe you have some deep-seated, atavistic complex—'the ghetto Jew' who, now that he's won full and equal rights, is struggling to be accepted by the gentiles. Ha!" Gherardo suddenly burst out laughing, "I hadn't thought of that—by the 'gentiles'! And you found yourself a family named Gentile!"

"I don't think it's so funny," I replied darkly.

"No, it isn't funny, I was just saying . . . maybe the fact that you're Jewish has nothing to do with it, who can say, maybe it's intellectuals like you who have complexes when they're in the society of the rich and powerful. As if they were saying, 'Can't you see how much knowledge I've acquired, how cultivated I've become, why don't you admire me at least a little bit?' But those people have absolutely no intention of admiring you. The things that you've acquired mean nothing to them. You have none of the things that really matter to them."

"That goes for you, too," I said, in an attempt to regain my footing.

"In a way it does, but not entirely. Don't forget that I belong to a family that has been rich and powerful for generations."

"That may be, you are rich, you are a free man. But explain something to me. Why on earth are you chasing after this family? You're a cousin, admittedly, but that doesn't really mean a thing. I don't think you're in love with any of the sisters. Then why do you pay calls on them so frequently? Why do you come to Rome, as if especially to see them?"

"*Touché*!" laughed Gherardo, "now it's your turn to catch me in my own contradictions. Why do I seek them out? I can't say. Perhaps it's because they are the only family I have . . . my mother is a character, a personality, but she is certainly more of a character than she is a mother. Could it be because they're nearly all good-looking? Perhaps. Don't forget that I am an aesthete, after all . . . I enjoy watching the three girls moving together up and down the halls of that apartment. And might it be because I feel a certain affection for them? It's conceivable, you can feel affection even for people for whom you feel no respect. Are there any maybes and perhapses you'd like to toss on the heap? After all, I was willing to do it for you . . ."

"Maybe it's because you're a sentimentalist," I ventured, with a smile.

"Who can say? Human degradation has no limits." Gherardo laughed with me, completely immune to the sting of the phrase I had launched in his direction, an expression that so deeply undermined his whole way of life and self-image.

By now Gherardo had calmed down and had turned back into the person he'd been in the first portion of our lengthy evening together. He asked me about Pindar and started making fun of me because of the exaggerated cult of heroes that typified "my" poet. "No different from Mussolini," he joked while I, resuming the manners and tics of a nitpicking professor, set out to explain to him, with growing warmth, that the sense of exaltation in Pindar was profoundly different from that of the Fascist regime.

Gherardo was driving calmly now, and as we progressed he asked me directions to the Albergo della Magnolia.

"I've been stopping for years at the Hotel d'Angleterre," he said to me, as if finding an excuse when we came within view of "my" hotel, but I reassured him with a wave of the hand.

Once again, we were speaking in calm tones; in fact, there was a sudden and heartfelt sense of fondness between us.

"Forgive me for the things I said," Gherardo said in a quiet, almost inaudible voice. "Take it for what it's worth . . . I'm too fond of paradoxes."

There was nothing to forgive, though. I waved goodbye and walked away.

Already the first pallid hues of dawn were beginning to sketch out the horizon, but what did that matter? In what remained of that night I didn't sleep at all.

# CHAPTER TWELVE

C lotilde and Renato Martini's wedding happened to fall on Yom Kippur, the solemn Jewish day of fasting. Of course, that was a pure coincidence, and no one had thought of it in advance, but for me—as you can easily guess— it was the cause of a degree of discomfort.

As I have told you before, Yom Kippur, along with the Passover Seder, was one of the two sole occasions over the course of each year in which I really felt Jewish. Although, that particular year . . .

Have you ever happened to stop and look at the central synagogue of Rome? It is a temple built around the turn of the twentieth century, and therefore it was designed to be massive and imposing, as if to shout with pride at the recent and successful emancipation of the Jews in Rome as well.

In case you're not familiar with it, let me tell you about it. That synagogue is not beautiful; neither is it evocative or mystical. It is as if someone one day gave a pile of money to a penniless child and said, as they shoved the child into a toy store, "Buy whatever you like." I can imagine that child throwing himself into a frenzy of toy-buying, chaotic and frenzied, without a glance back or a second thought.

Likewise, in that temple, my joyful ancestors threw in everything they could think of, a bit of Hellenism and a smattering of Asia, Doric and Ionic columns with ornamentation in perfect Assyrian style (Ruben liked to call it "Assyro-Frascatan"), and there were star-studded skies in azure and gold, palm trees and cedars and anything else that caught the eye of the beggar child in the toy store.

To come back to the topic at hand, I will add that the women's gallery (you may know that in Jewish liturgy women must be separated from men in the place of worship) in this monumental structure had been raised so impossibly high, practically bumping up against the golden stars, that it was difficult—no, simply impossible—for them to communicate even with gestures with the male half of the family.

That was why every family selected a tree all their own on the sidewalk running along the banks of the Tiber. Yes, that's right, a specific tree, the same one year in and year out, where men and women of the same family could finally come together without being obliged to wander in search of one another in the mob that flowed chaotically out of the synagogue, after the blast of the Shofar marked the end of Yom Kippur.

We, too, had a tree of our own. I still remember which one it was, the third tree along the riverbank, offset somewhat into the sidewalk, its roots breaking the surface like a weathered wrinkly hand.

Let's be clear on this point, I'm not trying to put together a set of nostalgic memories of questionable taste. It wouldn't even be a sincere reflection of who I was at the time. I went to that tree because I had decided to do so. I had said yes to Yom Kippur and no to many other things. I wasn't uncomfortable being there, in the midst of the clamoring extended family, but I wasn't all that deeply involved either. As always, what came to the fore was my sense of being a spectator in the presence of life, though one who was willing to vary the setting or the background and to witness panoramas that were not my own.

To return to us and that particular year . . . How could I venture, that year, to wait nonchalantly next to the usual tree, if Aunt Esterina was refusing to speak to me and Ruben had vanished from my life?

I had already told my mother that I couldn't bring myself to wait outside the temple as if nothing had changed. I had cautiously added the proviso "for the time being," and perhaps I really believed in that "for the time being."

I vaguely imagined that my family would gradually calm down, that is, that with the passing of time, matters would settle down of their own accord.

But I hadn't known—when I talked with my mother—that the day of Yom Kippur would be the same as Clotilde's wedding day.

I couldn't imagine that, instead of being at the synagogue, I would find myself in the midst of a solemn Roman Catholic mass being sung in the magnificent church of Santa Maria del Popolo and that afterward, instead of fasting, I would be standing with a glass in one hand, surrounded by a crowd of people dressed in their finest clothes, amidst the sumptuous carpets and wall hangings of the Hotel de Russie.

My father and mother had been dutifully invited, but they had managed to come up with a fully persuasive excuse not to attend. To be exact, it was my mother who had taken care of the details, saying to me, "After all, it's none of their business what we choose to do, is it?" with a rancorous and irritated tone that I had never heard in her voice before. Then she asked me, in a neutral tone of voice, "You're going, aren't you?," but she must have taken the answer for granted, because she turned and left without waiting for me reply.

Of course I had to attend. In fact, I *wanted* to attend. It had been planned that my presence at the wedding would be, as it were, "official," a sort of public presentation for anyone who hadn't already met me. A presentation that would substitute for the engagement party that had never taken place.

And so while my father, my mother, Aunt Esterina, and who knows how many other Jews around the world, Jews I had never met—some out of faith, others out of tradition, or driven by superstition, some in full awareness, others out of habit, some deeply moved and others chattering away about business and money—spent their day of fasting, I was carefully knotting my silvery necktie above my formal suit, inspecting myself in the mirror to be sure that I was perfectly dressed, and then walking rapidly over to the Piazza del Popolo, ready to stride through the portal of the church, where the organ was already working through the opening notes of Gounod's "Ave Maria."

What did I feel deep down? Well, to tell you the truth, practically nothing. After all, it is each of us that charges certain phases or events of our lives with symbolism and significance. One need only choose not to carry out this or that mental operation. It is sufficient to double-lock your front door and forbid certain primitive and, in the final analysis, all-too-obvious sensations from flowing chaotically through us . . . In other words, it is sufficient to become pure and rational thought alone.

And so I was walking and thinking . . . there were so many aspects of human life to think about without being overwhelmed by troublesome incidental problems. I had flipped the switch to off and I had muffled any chaotic internal impulses. I was walking rapidly, and I even felt a little giddy by the way I was moving confidently, a purely rational, clear-thinking human being.

As I arrived outside of the church, I stood there for a moment, bewildered at the sight of so many people. The broad buoyant hats worn by the women, the flowing lines of their outfits in an infinitely varied spectrum of pastel hues, the patches of dull grey and lustrous sheen of the gentlemen's formalwear. People hunting for other people, greeting one another, flashing smiles.

As I stood there trying to get my bearings, I felt someone companionably take my arm.

"Hey there, here we are." It was Gherardo, a competitor in the universal parade of elegance and, I must say, a competitor who stood head and shoulders above the run of the mill. His "we" sounded slightly exaggerated, since Gherardo was completely alone.

"You see, they chose this church just for you," he grinned immediately with a conspiratorial air. As I stood there, looking at him with a baffled expression, Gherardo burst out laughing. "Hey! Snap to! Isn't this the church with the painting of the conversion of Paul on the road to Damascus? One of Caravaggio's finest works. Did you forget?"

Perhaps I had forgotten, or perhaps I'd never seen that canvas by Caravaggio. Still, Gherardo . . . We'd seen each other many times by now, and we had become friends, but Gherardo just couldn't resist unleashing his caustic and slightly vicious wit on whoever came within range.

The conversion. It was a dumb joke. But to bring it up on that of all days . . .

I wasn't particularly tense because it was Yom Kippur, I already told you that. Still, there were reasons I couldn't bring myself to feel comfortable.

During our first meeting, I had promised Giuseppe Gentile that I would never let family and friends know that I wasn't Catholic, but here, in the midst of all the pomp and circumstance of a religious ceremony, would I be able to behave properly?

Of course, my future father-in-law had subtly dropped the hint now and again that I wasn't a practicing Catholic, but it was one thing not to be particularly religious, quite another to be entirely ignorant of the words and gestures of Catholic ritual.

"Imitate me, do as I do," Sonia had whispered to me, as if she were able to read my mind. As always, Sonia appeared at my side at just the right time and in just the right manner. This was what was so wonderful about Sonia; equally wonderful was her beauty on that day of celebration, a beauty that was pliant, a beauty that could be shaped like warm wax, adapting itself to the various occurrences that life brought. That day, her eyes harmonized with the highlights of her sky-blue outfit, a sky-blue that was echoed by a large flower perched on the crown of her hat.

The bride was quite another matter. When she entered the church on her father's arm, her hair drawn back and held snug under a bead-spangled cap from which trailed the long white veil, it was as if Venus herself had descended to earth to take a stroll.

But there was nothing more to it than that. Clotilde was like a message shouted at the top of one's lungs. You could hear the overwhelming sound, but you couldn't make out the individual words.

These vague words and images passed through my mind once again, while someone, I believe it was Sonia, led and gently pushed me toward a pew up front, in one of the first few rows, as was appropriate for the closest family members. On one side of me sat Sonia, of course, and on the other side was Lorenza, who I had seen arrive, to my great amusement, clomping along awkwardly in her very first pair of high-heeled shoes.

Now the ceremony had begun, and with it, like clockwork, my growing sense of uneasiness.

There was nothing I could do about it. I didn't fit in. I was struggling to keep from being conspicuous, but at the same time, I could barely bring myself to parrot gestures and mouth words that were so profoundly alien to me.

Perhaps because it was still a sultry October day, or perhaps not, in any case I found myself drenched in sweat.

It was just then that I felt a hand gripping my elbow, hard, and I turned around.

"Walk me outside . . . I don't feel well." Lorenza's face was ashen, and she looked miserable. She looked as if she were on the verge of fainting.

Her mother heard noises behind her; turning around, she spoke to me. "What's the matter?" she was whispering, practically without moving her lips. Under my breath I told her that Lorenza wasn't well, that there was nothing to worry about, I'd see her out of the church.

We walked out, doing our best to attract as little attention as possible, but in vain. Lorenza's new high heels, striking hard on the marble floor, seemed to prompt an infinite succession of echoes, and the fact that she was slumping onto my shoulder awoke a certain uneasy curiosity among the audience, which immediately turned to watch us leave.

"She's overcome with emotion, poor child!" murmured a matron wearing a hat shaped like an onion, and the gazes of the crowd filled with understanding and concern.

The minute we were out of the church, Lorenza seemed to feel better. She was no longer leaning heavily on me; in fact she was standing up straight and walking easily. The fresh air must have done her good.

"Come on, let's go get something to drink," she said to me in a voice that was hale and hearty, to say the least. "I want to sit down and take off these damned heels for at least five minutes."

"You . . . how do you feel?" I asked her in some astonishment.

"Me? I feel perfectly fine."

"What about before? I mean, you felt sick in the church, didn't you?"

"I've never felt better." Lorenza had resumed her off-putting persona. "I'm just a talented actress. After I finish high school, I want to go to acting school."

"Well, you fooled me; I never suspected a thing," I replied with some annoyance. "I'd like to know why you put on that ridiculous act, and in front of a crowd like that."

By this time, we had reached a little outdoor café at the far end of the piazza, and Lorenza had dropped onto a chair. She quickly unlaced her shoes and, with two sharp kicks, she was barefoot.

"A rhubarb cordial!" she called out to the waiter, without asking me to order for her; I was her escort, after all. I felt obliged to say, "I'll have one too," even though I don't like rhubarb cordial at all.

"Why did I do it?" Lorenza answered in a placid tone of voice. In the meantime, she had picked up one of her shoes, grasping the strap between her toes, amusing herself by dangling it precariously in midair. "Why did I do it? For you, of course."

"For me?!" This girl enjoyed startling me continuously, and I didn't like it a bit.

"Listen," Lorenza said, her voice suddenly serious and cutting. "Do you know Catholic religious ceremonies? No, you don't. So you didn't know that in about two seconds, everyone else in the church was going to kneel, and you were going to have to kneel with the rest of them . . . Or else stand there, alone, sticking out like a sore thumb, with every idiot in the church staring at you open-mouthed like a school of fish."

"You did it for me." I was no longer asking; I was simply acknowledging the fact in amazement. I sat speechless for a long time.

Lorenza. Lorenza was just like Gherardo. There was someone else in that family who was watching me, judging me. But Lorenza had also tried to help me, while Gherardo mostly seemed to enjoy stinging me, mocking me.

Then something odd happened. I had passed unharmed through the turmoil of a trying day and only now, at that exact moment, did I realize how acute was the pain of my situation. I felt in an inexplicable and absurd way as if I were precisely what I wasn't, a penniless Jew from some ghetto, obliged by history to hide, to seek camouflage in the society that rejects him. And all of this just because a young girl had tried to help me.

"And so," I murmured after a moment's silence, "I even owe you a debt of gratitude."

"Oh, I did it because I felt like it. I hate those masquerades, everyone standing around dressed to the nines . . ."

Heavens above, the worst mistake I could have made was to express gratitude to a girl like Lorenza, a girl who fought nail and tooth to ward off any hint of sentimental foolishness.

"No, you did it because you have a kind heart, and you're capable of understanding more than might at first appear," I insisted, all the same.

"Of course I understand. I'm sixteen years old. And I'm not a classical monument, unchanging through the ages. Time passes for me too."

Now Lorenza was amusing herself by taking small, angry, barefoot kicks at her shoes, abandoned on the floor, just the way that Ruben had kicked at the piles of rain-drenched leaves that evening so long ago (at least it seemed to me that a long time had passed since then).

Suddenly it dawned on me that the only way to placate Lorenza was to stop trying to be funny and talk to her as an adult. I discovered, to my amazement, that I wasn't doing it just for her. I soon felt very comfortable engaged in a serious discussion with that young woman who might be a little disjointed in her behavior, but who was also mature and penetrating in her judgment. And so I practically forgot that Lorenza had just turned sixteen, and that it was pure chance that she wasn't a student in one of my classes.

We talked eagerly and happily for a long time. Then Lorenza turned playful again. She explained to me what she described as her atheism, and she assured me that if she ever decided to marry—which she seriously doubted—I would certainly have no need for anyone to pretend to feel unwell to rescue me from a church ceremony. In other words, there were no churches in Lorenza's future.

After a long while of this, realizing with some alarm that we had allowed far too much time to pass, I begged her to slip her feet back in those poor mistreated shoes.

Fortunately, we arrived at the very moment when the bride was walking down the red-carpeted steps, arm-in-arm with that lustrous young man she had just acquired as a husband.

"Are you all right? How do you feel, child?" Mother, sisters, and various unfamiliar relatives were clustering around Lorenza, who produced a queasy but courageous smile.

"You see," Signora Adelaide said to me afterward as she thanked me in a lukewarm manner for the way I had looked after her daughter, "Lorenza tries to act like a shameless young delinquent, but she's even more sensitive than the others. Look how moved she was at the sight of her sister getting married!"

# CHAPTER THIRTEEN

T he only shadow that darkened the wedding party—ever so slightly, because it turned out perfectly in every other detail—was that the mother of cousin Gherardo, the Contessa Gaia Colonnesi, chose not to favor her relatives with her much desired presence. A bout of rheumatic pain that afflicted one of her legs prevented her from walking comfortably, the contessa informed the family; moreover, the demanding process of harvesting that year's vintage made it necessary for her to remain on her estate.

Two excuses—Aunt Esterina always used to say, and perhaps it was a more widely shared opinion—two excuses wind up murdering one another, even in a case where both excuses happen to be true. But that both, or even one, of the Contessa's excuses were true was something that Signora Adelaide doubted very much.

"She made me look like a fool," she brooded relentlessly, "with Renato's family, and they're quite important themselves, you know . . . his father is the *Federale* of Rieti . . . and what must my ladies think?!"

I forgot to tell you that Sonia's mother was a member of a committee, a ladies' auxiliary association, the Ada Negri Circle, which spread a thin veneer of culture and a much thicker layer of society doings over a sort of charity activity, in the tradition of the Ladies of Charity of St. Vincent de Paul, meant to assist in various ways those citizens who were poor—and they added the proviso—but honest.

For that year and all of the following year Signora Adelaide had actually been appointed chairwoman, and so she was especially eager to make a prestigious showing with the small group of women that made up the executive board.

It had been in fact to the members of the board, as well as the family of her son-in-law, that Sonia's mother had "pre-sold" the attendance of her cousin the Contessa. Her failure to attend had been a mortifying slap in the face, as if she had been called a liar in public.

One consolation that Signora Adelaide could set against that defeat, at least as far as the Ada Negri Circle was concerned, was the prestigious achievement of having obtained from my mother, entirely free of charge, the use of the ballroom of the Albergo della Magnolia for the annual winter benefit auction of the creations that the ladies had stitched, knitted, and crocheted for that occasion with great devotion, care, and patience.

In the past, the auction had always been held in the cavernous and drafty hall of the Casa del Fascio, bare of carpets and sofas, and comparable—most strikingly—to a a third-class waiting room in a small-town train station. A more elegant and worldly setting, Signora Adelaide had explained, would bring in a larger crowd and result in a more successful auction. Which would mean that the Circle would have more funds to help their needy beneficiaries.

As you can see, whether or not she was pleased at the prospect of kinship with my family, Signora Adelaide promptly snapped up the advantages that came with those family ties, assuaging her conscience with the knowledge that those advantages were not for her but for the "needy beneficiaries."

The other factor that helped Sonia's mother to calm her nerves to some degree was the performance of her youngest daughter. In the past, whenever her friends had come to call on her at home, Lorenza's displays of rudeness—she barely even spoke to the visitors—had caused her great embarrassment.

Now, at last, she had been able to show to one and all that her three daughters were a loving family, perfectly united, and that was a comforting development.

"My mother promised that to make up for missing this one, she'll come to Sonia's wedding," Gherardo had said with a smirk to his cousin, which of course only made things worse.

It had already been decided some time before that no one would be invited to Sonia's and my wedding, for evident reasons. The official explanation was that the bride and groom had decided to pledge their vows in a remote hermitage, in the presence of only their respective parents and best man and bridesmaid. The reception—to make matters perfectly clear—would be held at least five or six days later, while the honeymoon would be postponed—a disappointment, certainly, but life isn't a bowl of cherries.

Considering these complicating factors, the last thing anyone wanted was the presence of a relentless and difficult personality like Gherardo's mother.

Gherardo knew this perfectly well. But he loved nothing better than a game of cat-and-mouse, and he felt a childish delight in throwing his cousins into a state of panic, really just to keep his hand in. He had also taken great enjoyment from watching, seated comfortably as if he were watching a performance in a theater, the highs and lows of our matrimonial negotiations, and he certainly had no intention of missing out on the final and culminating act. So he declared: "I'm going to attend the Secret Ceremony." He had coined that emphatically caricatural description of our Pauline marriage.

Of course, Gherardo was welcome to come. He was increasingly becoming a member of our inner family circle.

He came to Rome on almost a monthly basis, "to let the Isotta-Fraschini stretch her muscles," he said, but I sensed that since I had joined the family he was more at his ease. I had sensed this some time ago and, to tell the truth, I found it somewhat flattering. You know, there really is no limit to human complacency and self-indulgence.

Giuseppe Gentile had also noticed this tightening of family ties, and all things considered, I believe it pleased him.

When Giuseppe Gentile asked his cousin about his growing number of visits to Rome, Gherardo had replied in a solemn voice, "Mussolini needs me!"

Dottor Giuseppe Gentile was on the verge of losing his temper once again and blurting out an angry "Cut that out!" Shifting his gaze, however, he saw that the housekeeper Anatolia was in the room. There she stood, with such an ecstatic and rapturous expression that the master of the house chose to remain silent, lapsing into a half-smile that had all the earmarks of a grimace.

And so—as I was saying—at the dinner table we talked with Gherardo about our wedding.

About my wedding with Sonia.

We talked about it in practical terms, focusing on dates and logistical issues, and the more they wrangled over the details, the more I could feel myself sinking into a surreal daze.

Can they be arguing like this over a dream, a dream that for so many endless days had seemed impossible? They used ordinary, normal words, but no word that was used to describe the two of us could be normal. Their cloud could not be the same as our cloud. The same words, when spoken by "them," whether they were the name of a street, the button on a suit of clothing, took on a different significance, lost their luster, shrank in size and meaning. Every word that exists on earth had been conceived only for the two of us, and anyone else that dared to use that word could be nothing more than a usurper. I looked at Sonia and Sonia looked at me, and nothing more was necessary, all the rest was noise.

And yet they kept on talking. As I said, the dates were also scrutinized intently. As I heard them talk about days and months, I plummeted back into the world of concrete reality for a moment.

"Not in October, please!" I called out. No one asked me why. Signora Adelaide had ruled out November after some thought; that was the month of the dead; also December, which is the month of holidays, and then decreed that a wedding in January (referring of course to the January of the following year, and not the upcoming and all-too-close January of 1931) would be a daring and original choice.

I remember that among those present at this final and perhaps defining discussion were Clotilde and Renato, back from their honeymoon, a voyage that had taken them to Vienna, primarily in order to admire and enjoy the performance of the Lipizzaner stallions.

Gherardo had done his best, in vain, to obtain any details, however rudimentary, about St. Stephen's Cathedral, the Hofburg palace, or anything else. Renato and Clotilde both looked at him with some slight annoyance and then went back to their descriptions of the stallions and their magnificent acrobatics.

Yes, horses were an important element of their love story. Renato, just before their wedding, gave his bride-to-be a surprise gift of a bay that would be stabled for her on the family estate on the Via Salaria, right next to Renato's horse. Her horse answered to the unsurprising name ("In fact, I'm not surprised," Gherardo said to me immediately) of Fulmine, or Thunderbolt.

Clotilde reacted to the surprise her fiancé had prepared for her in the usual manner. "Oh, how nice! Thank you!" she said, without moving a single facial muscle. Was she really pleased? Or was she bored with the gift? With Clotilde, it was never possible to guess what she was feeling. None of what Clotilde might think or feel ever seemed to be translated into a facial expression or a physical gesture. With her, even the center of the lamp emitted utter darkness.

That evening there was another discussion.

You see, happiness is something that is so difficult to grasp. If you are in love, you have the happiness of your feelings, but is it a pure joy? It never was for me. I was aware that the river running through me was fed also by obscure underground streams consisting of anxieties, feelings of anguish, fears, incredulity, and even, in stretches, a cynicism that was capable of corroding even my finer feelings.

Then there is a more pedestrian happiness, linked to those external events that shape the banks of that internal river, while pulling flotsam and jetsam downstream with it. In other words, reality.

My success in winning permission to marry Sonia had brought me, as you well know, an immense joy, but also a great deal of bitterness. The achievement of our chance at love had not been without its shadows; indeed, there were quite a few.

That evening, however, was different. The problem in question was a practical one, certainly a specific matter, but this time it seemed to us that we had finally been endowed with a slice of untouchable, inalienable happiness.

By now you must be wondering what on earth I'm talking about. The answer will disappoint you; it was a simple proposal.

Giuseppe Gentile had promised to put an apartment in Sonia's name when we were married, just as he done for his eldest daughter. Well, Dottore Gentile suggested a trade. In fact, once Sonia left the apartment in the Via Borgelli, there would only be three people living there, and perhaps before long two people, because Lorenza was growing up as well. In short, our future—mine and Sonia's—was to have a growing family, while they, the Gentile family, would have a "shrinking" family.

And so what Giuseppe Gentile wanted was a smaller apartment for himself, but one that was closer to his bank, and to give us Via Borgelli 11. That's all.

But you realize what it meant? The house with the bougainvillea, the apartment with its private moon, the windows that I had spied upon from a distance during dozens of furtive nocturnal walks, dragging Ruben, who wanted nothing to do with that whole story . . . well, the apartment where I had imagined Sonia in my dreams would finally be ours. Life was giving me a gift of both the pearl and the oyster shell, together.

Can I tell you something? That evening I was happy. And Sonia too was very happy. Later, everything happened, but that evening, yes, I was happy.

I can't seem to remember where, when, and why it was that I decided to let someone open an account in my name.

Yes, there was a girl on the floor. She was stunningly beautiful. As I gazed at her, I felt that unmistakable thrill that tells you that what you're looking at is unique, once in a lifetime. And then she loved me too.

Later came everything else. There were parents, sisters, cousins . . . lost cousins, found cousins, and there was us.

There I was, looking at a crucifix in the chapel inside the Villa Borghese, a chapel composed of the shadowy and the exquisite.

I can remember clearly that I felt perfectly at my ease during that ceremony. It wasn't like the day of Clotilde's wedding. Here there was no need for me to hide, I didn't need to pretend or playact, there was no need for a sister, Lorenza, to come to my rescue by pretending she felt unwell.

Sonia, my beautiful Sonia, was receiving her sacrament and I was at her side, as I would be in other circumstances for the rest of our lives.

I watched her protectively, I was the spectator of her emotion, I had been the one who had rescued her happiness and carried it to safety.

Sonia sensed all this, and her subdued gratitude, it was plain to see, was wrapped up with her love.

"Interesting ceremony . . . I'd never seen one." My father said to me afterward, with his usual detached and imperturbable manner.

My mother looked as if her hair were completely disheveled, but in fact she had just been to the hairdresser.

There is just one more thing that I want to tell you about our wedding, or perhaps I should say, about the post-wedding. By now I'm tossing the dice on the table, and I want to go all the way.

At the time, no one could have imagined how the game would wind up, what combinations would prove important and which less so. And who can ever know in advance how the numbers of life will turn out?

We had been fluently happy the day of our wedding and during our honeymoon in Sicily, visiting the temples of Magna Graecia. And we were immediately happy there, in the apartment in the Via Borgelli, freed once and for all of the carved chairs and the doughnut-shaped armchairs.

Nowadays, with the sexual freedom of our times, it may be difficult for you to imagine this, but back then . . . back then it was hard to question the zeitgeist. In fact, we had waited for the bonds of marriage before consummating our love.

Once we crossed that threshold, however, nothing held us back and there was no shyness. Everything flowed as if we had begun to make love, rolling in passion on the grey-and-pink carpet of the Albergo della Magnolia, the very same evening we had been brought together by the whims of destiny, when I had barely touched her hand and she had responded and both of us felt something click into place.

Afterward, once we were in our own home, as was often the case with young brides in the old days, Sonia felt some discomfort, a slight case of inflammation. The truth is that the fact that she wasn't pregnant after two, much less three months of marriage was a source of alarmed concern.

The family doctor suggested she try a stay at the spa of Salsomaggiore. Yes, a refreshing, invigorating mineral water cure . . . sometimes Salsomaggiore was just the thing.

Sonia wasn't sure. I had school, Clotilde had her bridge tournaments, Signora Adelaide had to prepare for the big benefit ball in the spring. It was all a little trying. In contrast, a stay in an agreeable place, a place full of greenery and hydrotherapies, for the most part frequented by married women . . . really, all things considered, Sonia could go there by herself.

We were sorry to be separated, but after all, ten days would go by in a hurry.

As was often the case, it was cousin Gherardo who saved us from our uncertainty. "I'll come see you," he reassured Sonia, "it's a nice drive, and with the Isotta-Fraschini, I'll be there in next to no time." In fact, it was an opportunity to get out and about.

It really was a piece of luck to have a cousin who was wealthy financially but short of things to do, someone who liked to rush back and forth, in search of himself.

We wrote each other letters every day and when Sonia returned, her cheeks were ruddy and her head was humming with the aria from Mascagni's "Iris."

The old doctor had seen things clearly. Once she was able to relax and was more or less "cured," Sonia discovered that she was pregnant the next month.

# CHAPTER FOURTEEN

W e'll skip over six years of my life. We'll stop only briefly here and there, like seagulls that every so often set down briefly on the crest of the occasional wave.

I would have liked to tell you everything, and perhaps linger at length over certain details, but the fact is that I started to write to you not so you'd know about my life in general. No, that is not what drove me to write. I want and I must follow as the one crucial thread the disturbances that turned me into the old man that I am now.

What happened in those six years? I could fairly answer you, "Practically nothing," if I adhere to the crucial thread that I mentioned to you.

As for everyday life, on the other hand, yes, those were years in which joy prevailed and seemed as if it would reign all powerful, perhaps for all time.

Well, first of all, in January of 1933 the child for which we had longed was born.

There Sonia was, and she was the very image of beauty and pain, that image that I had sensed in a flash of future when I saw her for the first time, suffering, on the carpet of the Albergo della Magnolia.

But now, at the end of a long and excruciating agony, there was our son, immediately ready to shout with all the strength of his sturdy little lungs.

We named him Michele. Michele—Michael, the biblical angel, comrade and mirror image of Gabriel, and also a great

saint. In other words, a name that was appropriate for all reli-
gions, and that also struck us as a nice name.

As Michele grew, he proved to be a smart and likeable child,
energetic the way children can be, but with his mother's gift, an
innate sense of harmony that emerged in every gesture and
action.

Even when he was very small, Michele liked to sit next to me,
silent and still, and watch as I worked on my texts.

"Can I see the book with the ants?" he would ask me sometimes. You understand? Michele didn't know how to read yet,
but he could already distinguish between letters, and he could
see that Greek characters were different from those in ordinary
books that he found lying around the house. And he called the
Greek letters "the ants."

When I would hand him a text with "the ants," Michele
would look at them patiently, for a long time, and I thought
(though perhaps I was mistaken) with a special satisfaction.

Sometimes I took him with me to the Albergo della Magnolia, and he amused himself by running up and down the stairs
on the lower floors, something that had been strictly forbidden
to me when I was a child.

"When I grow up I want to have a house like Grandpa and
Grandma's," he said to me. "Our house doesn't have as many
rooms."

I fell for it. I am inflicting upon you the long-ago prodigies
of a child, entirely forgetful that nobody is interested in those
prodigies, no one but parents and grandparents profoundly
convinced that they are unique and astonishing. Nothing is
unique, this I know, and not even our feelings are "unique," but
it's equally true that no one can help but believe that their own
emotions really are.

The Albergo della Magnolia. I often went back in those years
to the Albergo della Magnolia.

My father, with the shyness that he invariably showed whenever he found himself obliged to discuss personal matters, had told me, shortly after my wedding, that . . . well, in other words, the idea that all I should bring home was my salary as a teacher, in comparison with Sonia's income . . . struck him as neither fair nor dignified.

The Albergo della Magnolia would be mine one day, and so it only seemed reasonable that I should begin to enjoy some of the profits, unless, of course . . .

Unless of course I wanted to start working at the hotel a few hours every week, so that a gratuitous revenue could be transformed into a proper salary.

You see how odd life is? I knew that it was a source of concern to my parents that I had nothing to do with that hotel, and that they wanted me to run it one day. This was the source of their desperate attempts to involve me, however marginally, in the operation of the hotel.

But you know exactly how things turned out. Both the hotel and the magnolia vanished into thin air, and what purpose was served by all of their worrying, all of their scheming? Other plans were being made for us, elsewhere and by others.

In any case, I had accepted, and willingly, the "work" solution. Two or three afternoons a week I would go to the hotel and busily take care of correspondence or anything else my father asked me to do.

Above all, though, I listened to my father, who seemed very eager to talk to me about his issues at work.

In those conversations, my father was no longer uncomfortable; in fact, while he explained his worries and we talked about them, he appeared extraordinarily lucid and animated. And then, ever since 1933, when Hitler took power in Germany, my father had begun to worry about politics. He would talk and talk to me, still lucid but no longer animated.

My father was the recipient of secret information with a

much greater wealth of detail than was available to most people, I believe brought to him by refugees who washed up at the hotel; he spoke their language.

I saw emaciated foreigners moving around with vague jobs in the kitchen or in the gardens in the courtyard, and my father seemed increasingly upset.

He wouldn't talk with me about these foreigners, especially because after a while they would vanish, and shortly others might take their place.

"Dad, it is true that Hitler admires Mussolini," I said, reminding him to calm him down. "But the reverse is absolutely not the case. In fact, Mussolini scorns his German junior partner, and he has even scoffed at his hatred for the Jews as a 'racial delirium out of keeping with the Italian spirit.'"

My father listened to me, and for a few minutes he took heart, but then he started shaking his head again. "What matters in a dictatorship is the dictator, and the dictator can change his mind in the blink of an eye."

It had seemed that my father was right when a clearly orchestrated anti-Jewish campaign began in the Italian press in 1934, but then, in no more than a month, the campaign vanished into thin air. Mussolini backtracked and, embracing the Zionist Goldmann, he had said: "I too am a Zionist."

"You see?" I said to my father, but he just shook his head.

When I returned home I would tell Sonia a little something about these conversations with my father, but even as I left the Albergo della Magnolia, and with the serenity that I felt as soon as I rejoined Sonia, all those problems seemed to shrink into the distance, as if they no longer affected us.

And yet I was happy with those weekly visits to the Albergo della Magnolia. I liked returning to the half-light, the blooming tree, the silent drawing rooms in the afternoon hours, the stairway with the red carpet runner which led to mysterious people and mysterious lives. The enchantment of my childhood came rushing toward me every time, like an overenergetic puppy. That was where I had been born and it was only there, like it or not, that I could find my traditions.

Traditions. I had understood something—I know, it's pretty simple, but even the simplest things have to be understood from the inside out. There are no traditions that are more significant, more deeply moving, or more enchanting in one religion rather than in another.

I had celebrated more than one Christmas with the Gentile family, I had been one of them, I had given and received presents handsomely wrapped in red and gold paper. I hadn't disliked it, I too felt myself immersed in that cheerful and comforting atmosphere, made up of light, Christmas carols, stars of Bethlehem, and chiming bells.

But it wasn't my holiday. I wasn't born to it.

What continued to matter to me was the sugar candy in my pocket to break our fast immediately after the sound of the shofar (if you waited till you got home, the wait was too long) and the last word in the last blessing of the Passover Seder, the Hebrew word *yochluhu*, which we children would stretch out in play, seeing how long we could drag out the final "u."

What is so fine about a sugar candy or a long, drawn-out "u"? Nothing. Perhaps a crèche is more evocative than a drawn-out "u," but that's not the point. It's not a question of a more or less persuasive religious symbol, you understand? It's about childhood, and you can't change childhood.

That, despite everything, was why I was beginning to suffer from my extended absence from the ceremony of Yom Kippur.

As I told you before, I hadn't gone to the synagogue the year that Clotilde was married; nor had I gone the following year. Sonia was pregnant and I didn't want to leave her by herself.

But they were all just excuses. The real reason was the wall that now separated me from the rest of the family. I wasn't eager to plunge into the crowd and run the risk of being snubbed and humiliated.

The following year—yes, it was the year after, 1933, and I remember that because of the unsettled conversations I had begun to have with my father—on Yom Kippur I felt uneasy, as if I were driven to seek out some remaining shred of family atmosphere.

I was upset when I left the house. In truth I only wanted time to walk and think. Then I turned down the street that leads to the neighborhood of the Main Temple. I had no intention of even looking inside. I only wanted to walk in that general vicinity and hear, perhaps at a distance, the sounds and songs that were issuing—not even particularly muffled—from the great stained-glass windows.

I was cautiously staying on the far sidewalk, beneath the line of plane trees overlooking the river, and I had chosen an inter-mediate afternoon hour, before the inevitable rush of crowds to attend the holiday's closing ceremony.

I was walking along in a tranquil state of mind, a state verging on serenity. I remember that it was a particularly mild autumn; it still almost felt like summer. The sky was clear, there was just a hint of a breeze. Only scattered shreds of fluffy clouds crept overhead and then fled rapidly, like children in pajamas who sneak downstairs to peer in at the guests at a grown-up party.

In that air, under that sky, I met Ruben.

It was an unusual hour for him as well, and he was walking, all alone, on the same side of the street, along the river, but in the opposite direction.

We came to a halt, one facing the other, and looked at each other without a word—time dragged out, it seemed, inter-minably.

"What are you doing here?" Ruben's unhurried voice was the first to break the silence.

"I was taking a walk," I replied in the same tone of voice.

"Oh really?" and Ruben almost imperceptibly turned his head, ever so slightly toward the big brightly lit synagogue.

"I married Sonia." I said to him after a pause.

"I know."

"I have a son named Michele."

And Ruben said to me again: "I know."

We spoke these few words, but it was as if the silence still extended between us, a silence charged with emotions we wanted to keep under the surface.

"Now I live at Via Borgelli 11, did you know that?" I asked him after a moment.

"No, that I didn't know. Do you live with your in-laws?" and Ruben smiled ironically.

"They moved out . . . they left it to us," I said, this time a little breathless.

"Congratulations!"

I had sensed in him a certain degree of detachment. I was losing Ruben once again, and I couldn't stand that.

"I told you that I live in Via Borgelli because I'd really like it if you came to see us . . . yes . . . to meet my son . . ." My voice was at once emphatic and anxious, and there filtered through, despite my best efforts, a tone of supplication.

"I'll think about it," Ruben said to me, and looked at me one more time before walking slowly across the road running along the Tiber.

Three days later the doorbell rang at my house.

And so everything started up again with Ruben, just as before.

Not exactly the same as before, because we had also resumed the tradition of meeting in the street and taking long walks with long conversations, but more frequently, nowadays, it was Ruben who happened by the apartment and, seated on one of our easy chairs, spent hours chatting with me and with Sonia.

At our house he often ran into Lorenza, as well, and occasionally Gherardo, who continued to run down to Rome practially every month.

Certainly he didn't spend all his free time with us.

The tradition of the family dinners at the Gentile home had not died out; indeed, it endured more triumphal than before. Over the years, the table had made room for new guests, since on special occasions the children were invited as well, Clotilde and Renato's two young twins (they had each received a gift pony) and our own Michele. There was room for everyone, and then some. The truth was that, with his new apartment, Giuseppe Gentile hadn't retrenched at all, the way he had suggested to us that he was planning to do. Quite the opposite. Perhaps there were one or two fewer bedrooms in the apartment, but the living room was much larger than the one in the Via Borgelli, and it also boasted a sizable terrace with plants and trees which lent itself generously in terms of extra space.

Lorenza, once she obtained her high school diploma, insisted at all costs on enrolling at university, triggering a predictable fit of consternation from the family.

"A woman with a college degree? No one will ever marry you!" moaned Signora Adelaide, while her husband, pacing nervously back and forth across the big room, gestured emphatically as he recalled what Mussolini had stated unequivocally on more than one occasion.

"Let us leave female ministers and parliamentarians to other nations," the Duce had declaimed. "We want our women to stay home and take care of our children—in other words, we want them to be women."

"In other words," and here Dottor Gentile hesitated for a moment, "it has been scientifically proven that women are less intelligent, and so . . ." However, Giuseppe Gentile was unwilling to venture beyond that allusive "and so," because, like everyone else in the family, he was slightly afraid of Lorenza. What made matters even worse was the fact that Lorenza hadn't chosen to enroll in the department of literature where she could eventually set out on a reasonable female career as a teacher; no, she had stubbornly insisted on enrolling in the school of medicine. Medicine was what she wanted, and medicine is what it would be.

"Come on," Gherardo had said. "Lorenza will wind up taking care of the lepers in Africa. Aren't you pleased, Adelaide, since you think that charity is such a magnificent mission?" Adelaide shuddered.

I also did my best, albeit with more rational arguments, to strike a blow on Lorenza's behalf, and with greater warmth so had Sonia, while her sister Clotilde rolled her eyes heavenward (already for her this was an extreme manifestation of her opinion).

In the end, as we all expected, Lorenza had her way and stubbornly began studying medicine.

Whenever she managed to tear herself away from her textbooks, she hurried over to our house to play with little Michele. Then, after a reasonable interval, she'd wander over to the living room and began talking animatedly with us. She'd do it if Ruben was there as well.

We talked about everything, but almost inevitably the topic turned to politics and remained there.

Let me make one thing very clear for you. Lorenza was a "disapprovant" of Fascism, but a much more vigorous and determined one than either of us. Ruben, too, with the passing years, struck me as more emphatic on this point, and the two of them really led the discussions, while Sonia and I increasingly played the role of timid bourgeois parents, stuck on the same repetitive refrains.

Whenever Gherardo was there, we ridiculed the Fascists

and made biting, sometimes brutal jokes at their expense, but none of us ever ventured any further. Perhaps we distrusted him instinctively, or maybe it was because we felt sure that the same darts that Gherardo tossed at the Fascists he would just as happily have aimed and vigorously launched at the anti-Fascists.

Why had I failed to understand it, or really I should say, when did I understand it?

I assumed that they just had different ways of expressing their ideas, but, in fact, at a certain point (when exactly had it been?), Lorenza and Ruben went beyond us and ventured onto the terrain of militant anti-Fascism. It was still strictly small stuff, of course, like leaflets or some clandestine publishing, but they were actually doing something. Sonia and I, in contrast, remained on the safer side of the stream.

This may be why in the second part of my life I chose to launch myself into the midst of all the wars that were fought to defend my new country. Now, however, these thoughts matter little or not at all . . .

I was telling you about Lorenza. I later guessed that Lorenza was probably a member of some secret committee at the university (it was probably there that her eyes had been opened), while Ruben I couldn't say, perhaps with her, or maybe elsewhere. It is the one thing that neither of them ever told me, and I've tormented myself over the years for having failed to understand it.

Let me do my best to be clear on this point. Even if I had known it, I could have done nothing to alter the course of events, nor for that matter was their anti-Fascist activism decisive in determining their destiny or that of anyone else. Things went the way that history chose to shape them.

My regret, therefore, is purely one of not having understood, of having failed to be close enough, affectionate enough.

To have cared so much about these people, to have practically lived with them but still failed to see, to sense . . . It's a bitter realization of the limitations of love.

Yes, love. Lorenza loved me, and she showed it in that rude and aggressive way of hers. It almost seemed that criticizing me and being mean to me was how she felt most comfortable expressing her affection.

Once Signora Adelaide had asked me to come deliver a lecture to "her ladies." I went to the Ada Negri Circle and I went on passionately about the Greek lyric poets, while the women in the audience interrupted me periodically to ask: "What about Sappho, professor?" When I finally got to Sappho I could almost hear a general sigh of relief.

Lorenza was intensely annoyed by my willingness to cooperate, which in her view went hand-in-hand with Sonia's tractability whenever there were major events and she helped her mother by serving as a kind of private secretary. Lorenza mocked Sonia, calling her "the good daughter," but with me she went much further than that.

She harshly scolded me for my "unnatural and therefore highly obnoxious" behavior when I interacted with the family as a group.

It was more or less the same thing that Gherardo had said to me, couched in different words, except that with Gherardo it seemed that the matter ended there, after the initial blowup. Gherardo and I never again discussed the topic that we had argued about so animatedly the night that he dragged me up to the Janiculum in his Isotta-Fraschini.

At the time I was deeply wounded by his tirade. I sincerely believed that with the passing of time I had gradually developed a more relaxed and natural way of interacting with the Gentile family, and that this was one of the main reasons that Gherardo hadn't attacked me again.

And now here was this young sister-in-law taking as an article of faith the fact that I was far too subservient, far too amenable to the demands of her "revered" family. As a result, I plunged back into my self-doubt and lack of confidence.

At first I was astonished at the way that Lorenza seemed to think she could just start scolding me with such ferocity, as if I were her little brother, a Pip that she had raised "by hand" (as if she were a Roman variant of *Great Expectations*' Mrs. Joe), even though I was her brother-in-law, practically a stranger to her, and much older than her, come to think of it.

In time I became accustomed to it, and later still, I was deeply moved. Lorenza, skipping any normal intermediate phases, treated me immediately as if I were her brother, and she had given me the impetuous gift of her affection, along with the rather rude manner of its manifestation.

In fact, after these attacks, whether they were intentional or involuntary, Lorenza calmed down, and started laughing and chatting with me as if nothing had happened. Indeed, as far as she was concerned, I came to understand, nothing had really happened at all.

In my childhood, Ruben had been my brother-friend, and now what survived of Ruben was the friend, and I had Lorenza as my sister.

This new wave of affection flowed within me, practically rendering my blood richer and more vigorous.

Sonia would sometimes look at us with a hint of consternation. I realized that she was in a state of anguish whenever she saw her little sister attack me so forthrightly and aggressively, but Sonia was equally mystified by the aftermath of those attacks. And so she seesawed from fear that I had been mortified to bewilderment at seeing us happily chatting away together, as if angry words had never been exchanged.

Sometimes, with Lorenza I found myself digging deep into my personality. There were times when I wondered whether this troubled intimacy of ours didn't in some sense undermine my relationship with Sonia.

I had no doubt that the answer was "no." Whenever Sonia and I talked about ourselves, there was a point beyond which we did not venture. Relentless honesty is an enemy of love. At a certain point with Sonia, there emerged the vagueness, the mysterious and contradictory nuances that represented the very warp and woof, the fabric of love itself.

Without light and darkness, without the chiaroscuro of dawn and the shadows of sunset, the sun alone would not be enough to make the flowers bloom.

# PART TWO

# CHAPTER FIFTEEN

It's been a few days since I wrote anything. I needed a break, I needed to catch my breath and gather my strength before we began our descent. A descent that will take us down to the general vicinity of hell, whatever meaning each of us chooses to assign to that overused image.

Yes. Hell. Forgive me if no other word seems to come to mind for the moment.

As I've pored over these sheets of paper, writing and re-reading, the months have gone by. From that glowing June of the six days of war we have moved on into a dry and scorching summer and then, little by little, the season has begun to decline.

Autumn has come and it has brought with it, as it does every year, what we call the "autumn holidays." Our New Year and, once again, the fast day of Yom Kippur.

Where am I now, in relation to the great punctuations of Jewish life? Am I still a "twice-a-year" Jew? It's hard to say.

When I was living among the rocks, in the kibbutz of the pioneers, we all declaimed an extreme and even a furious brand of socialism. We considered the religion of our fathers a symbol of the "old Jew," the kind of Jew who bows his head over his books, and then turn to bow his head before a tormentor who enjoyed the right to decide whether he would live or die.

And so, to offer an example, I can tell you that on Yom Kippur the creative cooks in charge of our meals would do their best to come up with the most tempting dishes imaginable (at least, compared with the usual fare) in an attempt to persuade the *chaverim*, the comrades, to forget about any temptations they might have had to fast.

Frequently this culinary seduction was successful, but in some cases it was not. Certain of our comrades, when the meal was served in the dining hall, would simply walk off distractedly into the fields, and you wouldn't see them again for a while.

Then, as you already know, I changed kibbutzim, and later still I moved to the city.

Here, in this country of ours, the difference between being religious and not being religious is less sharp. Yom Kippur is Yom Kippur for everyone. You can sense it in the street, you can see it stamped on the faces of your neighbors. You walk and you know that the clusters of people you encounter are walking to temple or leaving a temple, while many others that you meet are walking along, indifferent or focused on other things, chattering to one another and laughing, and they don't even bother to look up when they walk past a synagogue . . .

But none of that matters. It's the same sky, and the sky belongs both to you and to those who are chattering and laughing. If you don't feel like committing yourself personally, you can always pilfer something from the others. To venture a metaphor, and not a particularly appropriate one since we are talking about fasting, I would say that at this great general banquet, everyone can enjoy a morsel or two by taking it from their neighbor's plate.

When my parents were alive, I would come to the city to see them and I'd more or less celebrate the holidays with them. We saw one another so infrequently back then. Now an old colleague of mine invites me over for the holiday; he's a teacher of ancient Greek like me, but at another high school. He's a professor of German origin, and he has white hair and a quiet and courteous wife who reminds me of other times, other atmospheres . . .

They aren't very religious themselves, but we fast, and we drink a lukewarm broth when the fast is over (no sugar candies; old age has blunted our eagerness).

I don't know exactly when and how they escaped from Germany. Here, as I've mentioned, people tend to avoid talking about before. For that reason, but also out of patriotism, many of us have changed their first and last names, either by Hebraizing their own names or by taking advantage of some similarity of sound or else just inventing some new names out of whole cloth. But imagination must have been in short supply because, even among my own acquaintances, there is a series of Mordechais and Jehudas, so that it starts to feel as if I'm always talking to the same people.

I reached back for the surname of my Lithuanian great grandfather Katz, which sounds very old-world Yiddish, and I changed Dino to David. You might say I wasn't particularly original either, and you would be right.

It's fall already, I was telling you, and the weather has changed. The day before yesterday there was a sudden gale with gusting winds and, somehow, I'm not really sure how, the glass in the French door that leads onto the little balcony was broken. Then calm returned, and once again I could hear the cry of the owl that calls out questions in the night from the big tree on the boulevard.

When the glass broke, my cat Shulamit looked at me askance, as if she thought that I had deliberately shattered it into smithereens. The fact is that Shulamit is jealous when she sees that I'm writing to you. She must have figured out that the time I spend poring over these sheets of paper to you is something very different from when I focus on an essay or a letter to my fellow scholars.

And so, when she catches me seated at my desk in that certain stance (I'll never know exactly what she sees), she becomes grumpier than usual and for hours and hours she plays hard to get; she runs away when I call her. But I act as if everything's perfectly normal, and she gets over it eventually.

Now that we can finally touch the Wailing Wall, they come in droves, believers, doubters, and nonbelievers, to place their hand on the wall. I've noticed that some slip notes into the cracks between the ancient stones. Wishes, requests, appeals for hope, despairing phrases . . . who knows what's written on those scraps of paper. It never occurred to me to do that; instead I am writing to you.

And so we have glided over six years of happiness, and we are approaching the funereal year of 1938.

Funereal, and yet . . . That year, Michele had just turned five and sometimes talking to him was truly an amusing thing.

One day he was riding on the trolley with me, sitting quietly next to the window, when suddenly he asked me in a loud voice, "Does God eat ice cream cones?" I was embarrassed, not so much at the question, as at the fact that—I had noticed—every passenger on the trolley had turned toward us, curious to hear what answer I would give.

I can't remember anymore exactly what I said to him; I think I just gave some stock answer, and it's not really that important now. Instead I remember certain details from Michele's childhood. For example, I remember that Michele was strictly forbidden to eat ice cream cones, because Sonia would not allow our son to eat something purchased from an unsanitary ice cream cart—and Michele was tormented by this rigid rule.

Ice cream cones from an ice cream cart became the central myth of his childhood, and also the focus of his efforts to exercise the logical capacity for persuasion that he possessed, a capacity that was made stronger by a confident argumentation you'd expect from a young adult.

Perhaps many children were like that then, and are like that even now, but even now I am captured by it from time to time.

These glimpses of the past pop out suddenly, and I don't have the heart to tuck them back into the past. So please be patient with me.

At the beginning of that year of 1938 there burst onto the scene the new rule governing the use of the formal. Instead of using the antiquated form of *lei*, the new formal term of address was to be *voi*. A government order required all Italians to stop using the old form of address, and this sudden political purge of a manner of speech swept through society. There was even a women's magazine named *Lei*, and it was forced to change its title.

This laughable detail came to mind because I have a vivid recollection of one encounter with my father and mother-in-law.

As you know, Sonia's parents had always addressed me in the formal, using the old *lei*, and I used the same form in speaking to them. Now, suddenly, the new regulations of the Fascist regime had to be obeyed . . .

I never saw Giuseppe Gentile in such a bind as that day, as he explained to me that, after all, Mussolini was right, the *voi* was a more virile and a more Italian form of address, while the *lei* sounded foreign and servile. And therefore . . . still Dottor Gentile couldn't bring his monologue to a conclusion.

I had perfectly understood that he was gathering his courage to address me with the *voi*, but that he couldn't bring himself to do it, right then and there, without preamble.

"If we don't set an example for the others . . ." he had blurted out, and then stopped in his tracks. After that, for a good long while, when he spoke to me, he avoided using either *lei* or *voi*, relying on the Tuscan custom of using the impersonal, or veering off into complicated turns of phrase. His wife was more pragmatic. To avoid complications, she started using the informal, addressing me with the *tu*, and the decision to do so certainly did not spring from a sudden swell of affection.

Why am I telling you all this? Well, I know that these are details that, all things considered, belong to the realm of the grotesque, not the domain of tragedy, and are therefore very distant from the sense of the abyss that looms threateningly over my story.

But if I think back on it, I know that's not the way it is.

That funereal *voi*, unthinkable in at least half of Italy, the abolition of the handshake, replaced by a marionettish Fascist salute, the Blackshirt hierarchs who lumberingly leapt through hoops of fire, their sagging bellies barely clearing the flames, Germany annexing Austria, Hitler arriving in Rome, the city spruced up and decorated for the occasion, welcomed triumphantly by the King of Italy and by Mussolini . . . these were all flashes of sinister lightning against our sky, the leaden, deceptive tints of a painting that the mysterious hand of a painter was completing for all of us . . .

And at home, Giuseppe Gentile, adhering like a glued label to the wishes of the regime, chose, as the target of his practice of the new *voi* ordered by the Duce, chose none other than me, me before all others.

I'd never had any illusions. I had always sensed his hostility hovering over us.

Nothing served to lessen that distinct sense of hostility: not the stock phrase that he used to introduce me—"a future star of our university system"—not the admiring fondness that Gherardo openly felt for me, not the birth of my son, his grandson. In appearance, Giuseppe Gentile's consideration for me as a person seemed to include a degree of respect and esteem, but the adamantine core of his profound dislike persisted, endured tenaciously.

But now, after the prelude, we arrive at the first act.

I can't imagine how to convey to you the astonishment, bewilderment, sense of suffocating panic, and ultimately the despair that seized us, leaving us breathless, gasping. Because what only my father had imagined or guessed at in his dark fantasies, what none of us had been willing to believe, not even Ruben, not even Lorenza with her sensitive antennae, not even the militant anti-Fascists, and not even the most fearful Jews, those who had the clearest and most recent memories of the ghetto—well, at last it had happened.

"Manifesto of Racist Scientists" was the headline that appeared one day in July in a box on the front page of a newspaper. In the "Manifesto" we read that the Italians should openly avow their racism, that there was such a thing as a pure Italian race, and that "the Jews do not belong to the Italian race." In ordinary everyday words, they were expaining to us that the Jews should no longer consider themselves—or be considered—Italians.

How do I remember that July day? Do you really think that I could ever forget it?

In the middle of summer, with the school closed, I found myself wandering the streets. Then I had gone to the library and, walking home as I so often did, I stopped at a newsstand to buy a paper.

I don't know how I found my way home. Sonia was at home, and so was Ruben, sitting across from her.

Ruben was about to tell me what had happened, but he saw from the expression on my face that there was no need, that I knew everything too.

"Mussolini did it because Hitler asked him to, isn't that right?" Sonia asked anxiously.

"I couldn't say," Ruben replied, "but I doubt that Mussolini needed any advice or encouragement."

I had the distinct impression that Ruben must have said something of the sort to Sonia already, even before I arrived, but that Sonia had turned a deaf ear and continued to cling to her vague hypothesis, repeating it from time to time as a sort of ritual of consolation.

"If Mussolini ordered this new set of rules, it was his own decision," I broke in harshly. It was strange, but I felt that I had used my father's words and his tone of voice.

This time it was Ruben, perhaps moved to pity by Sonia's hopeless floundering, who tried to throw water on the flames. "Maybe it won't mean that much after all . . . it's just a document . . . a momentary stand . . . yes, it might have been influenced by a conversation with Hitler . . . but you know how things work in Italy . . . one rhetorical gesture, and then our beloved Duce has moved on to the next thing. This wouldn't be the first time."

And while Sonia was doing her best to work up a smile, I continued to feel as if I were split in two. It seemed as if deep inside me was my father, and I caught myself shaking my head the way he did, just the way he had shook his head five years before when, in 1933, Hitler had seized power and the Albergo della Magnolia had become a destination for a silent stream of mysterious messengers of distant calamities.

"I need to go to the Albergo della Magnolia!" I blurted suddenly, and left hastily, leaving Sonia and Ruben to look at one another in concern.

The Albergo della Magnolia was still there, as calm and comforting as ever, in the dim light filtering into the sitting rooms and halls through the dark heavy curtains. I was almost amazed at the sight. Lunch was already being served, and from behind the French doors came a subdued buzz and the faint clicking sounds of utensils and dishes being busily sorted and moved.

My father came out immediately. He looked pale to me, but absolutely impeccable in his dark suit. He looked at me silently for a moment, as if there were something he wanted to scold me for, but then all he said was: "I have to go. The hotel is filled with guests and it's lunch time; you know how demanding that can be."

He turned his back on me and left, dignified and composed.

As I was about to walk out the door, disturbed and, I admit, very disappointed as well, my mother ran after me.

"This will all blow over, won't it?" she asked me a little frantically. "Mussolini will change his mind just like he did four years ago, right?" She didn't give me a chance to reply. "Of course, here in Italy people say things and never follow through . . . " she reassured herself, and then hurried off because she too had hotel guests to look after.

That evening, without warning, Dottor Giuseppe Gentile came to see us. He just showed up, with no advance warning, and at a time when he was usually still in his office at the bank.

"Do you remember our conversation eight years ago or so?" he asked me in a grim tone of voice before I could open my mouth. "Now you see? I was right." Then he turned on his heels, kissed his daughter, and left.

The years have passed since them, so many other acts succeeded this one, and yet I still can't understand what my father-in-law was trying to say with that phrase, "I was right."

# CHAPTER SIXTEEN

In the middle of the summer, two more creaking sounds came to remind us that the platform we were standing on was gradually teetering close to collapse.

Every household received a census form and, on the newsstands, pride of place was assigned to a new magazine. *The Defense of the Race* was the name of the magazine, and it was being published for the sole purpose of fomenting hatred against the Jews, with grotesque articles and illustrations.

Ruben and I managed to hold the publication in our hands no longer than five minutes before tossing it into the rubbish where it belonged. What about others! How long would it take, how many hands would have to hold it before the magazine reached its intended audience?

There was no escape from the census. At the end of the list of customary questions, you had to state your religion, and then . . . Then, the next entry after "religion" was "race."

"You could lie, couldn't you? Who's going to know? Write 'Catholic,'" Sonia begged me, her anxiety emerging in spite of her best efforts.

Lie? No, it was too late to lie. When the question arose in 1930 of whether or not to enroll in the Jewish community, I had decided to enroll. I didn't want to lie.

None of us did, even though for each of us the same thing happened—our hands blocked, almost paralyzed, before writing "Jewish" next to the line marked "race."

Only Ruben had furiously written "white" and then hurled the pen angrily at the far wall of the room.

"Race." You see what I mean? We were no longer a religion, we were specifically identified by certain imaginary physical characteristics. Who had come up with this concept of a Jewish race, if it was no difficult matter to travel around the world and meet a blond fair-skinned Danish Jew and an Eastern Jew who had the Arab features of his neighbors?

What about the other Italians who had been obliged to respond "Aryan" under the heading "race"? Where did the idea come from that there was a shared Aryanness that linked Venetians and Sicilians, Ligurians and Calabrians?

Of course, there's no reason for me to waste time explaining to you how absurd that "scientific" contrivance had been. Nowadays, we can all look back on it and laugh, but I assure you that at the time . . . at the time, the more absurd it seemed, the deeper and more intense the scorching pain within.

And to think that it was such a lovely summer! August had always been a magical month for Sonia and me. Signora Adelaide took Michele with her to the seaside, near the Conero (her family owned land in that area), and we stayed behind in the shadowed rooms of the Via Borgelli. We could have gone away too, but for years we had chosen to spend August in that penumbra for two.

Thus, every August Sonia and I became the tenacious sculptors of our lives together.

We were happy. And before allowing myself to plunge into the darkness, let me recall for you (and for myself!), as in a last snapshot, some element of those happy days.

A scene, taken from any year, any year chosen at random.

For instance, the sense of liberty. The electrifying sensation that we could invent in absolute liberty the craziest schedules to live each day. We could sleep in until late, we could eat in bed the imperfectly cooked foods that we had prepared for ourselves in the kitchen, we could look out our window late at night, spying on our own private moon.

We imagined ourselves as prisoners of our apartment (and to some extent it was true, the heat held us prisoners), and we invented a thousand different ways to spend our time.

Sometimes I would read books aloud. Sonia liked it when I did this. She said that if we each read a different novel, we would plunge into two far-too-different worlds.

I remember that while I was reading *Zeno's Conscience* every so often she would break in, interrupting me to say, "But that's you . . . that's you to a T!"

Some time earlier she had exclaimed the same thing about Swann (if so, who would be my Guermantes family?) and so, laughing, I had replied to her, "You see me as every Jewish character in every novel we read!"

"No," Sonia had whispered, "not in every Jewish character, in every character, period. Because the only one that exists for me in the world is you, and for that reason, I see you everywhere."

Sometimes we would quarrel, but as a joke. I'd call her "Lady of St. Vincent de Paul," and Sonia would shoot back, "damned hotelkeeper!"

I never took offense, but Sonia did. She was horrified at the thought of being mistaken for her mother and she insisted each time the matter surfaced that the work she did helping children with their homework was something quite different from the charity revolving around a benefit ball.

When we got to that point, I'd call her my "little lady" or my "Vincentina," though it was just a prelude to a series of other terms of endearment.

In the evening we would go out, braving the heat of a movie theater, or else setting out in search of a trattoria in the working class neighborhoods of Trastevere or Testaccio. We would walk back home, hand in hand, and finally fall asleep in the early hours . . .

*

Then everyone would come back to town. Michele would come back, and we were certainly very happy to have him with us again.

And we too would come back. We'd go back to being the people we were before: my school, Sonia's activities, and the people she went out to meet.

Still, something always survived of that month. A sense of complicity. The shared secret of an interval of mad if subdued abandonment to the unchecked flow of our emotions, which we apparently kept safely stocked away for the following summer, but which remained as a symbol, as a living, pulsing cell that gave meaning even to our most ordinary days.

That's not how it was that year, I can assure you. Even Ruben had stopped trying to reassure Sonia. No, the "Manifesto of Racist Scientists" was not some spur-of-the-moment inspiration, destined to run its course and then vanish into thin air. At first, Ruben had half believed that, and had allowed Sonia to hope for the best, but not now, no longer. Now that a copy of *The Defense of the Race* was sitting on the dining room table (we couldn't keep ourselves from buying each new issue, and throwing it out almost as soon as we bought it), snickering at us, mocking us, with its images of Jews with hooked noses and small, piggish eyes, whispering to us, "You see, this conversation's not over, this conversation's going to continue."

We found ourselves trapped in an unpleasant interlude, but if we had one certainty, it was that the future was bound to bring something even more unpleasant.

In our living room, even when Ruben was there, there reigned a grim silence, and the words, when they did emerge, came out reluctantly, like the last few drops in the pipe of a dried-out faucet.

That year I missed the others, I wanted to be forced to dull my nerves with words and conversation. But every summer, Lorenza agreed for the month of August to "be a good daughter," and uncomplainingly followed her mother to Conero. Since Michele came onto the scene, this duty had been transformed into something more joyous.

What about Gherardo? I was eager to hear what Gherardo would have to say. Surely he would have something fiery to say, we all knew how eloquent Gherardo could be. His observations would bring some light to these dark days, even if I knew all too well how quickly his lightning was destined to vanish, echoing away in distant thunder in faraway skies.

Gherardo in fact was relaxing at Forte dei Marmi. He hadn't renounced his holidays on the Tyrrhenian coast since the day he was born, and he wasn't about to start missing them now.

And so the long-awaited period of solitude was only a burden to me that year. I couldn't stand sitting silently next to Sonia, but I couldn't keep from sitting in silence either.

At the time, I had no idea that this would be my last summer in that apartment.


Then Michele came home, Lorenza came home, and Gherardo came home, and he immediately turned around to come pay us a visit.

In September, there we all were, mourning over the coffin of someone or something dead, whose features we were not yet able to recognize.

And how could we fail to recognize those features? All we needed to do was look closely, take the time to observe . . .

At a certain point it appeared, no, we learned it for certain, that the Grand Council had issued its decree. Yes, it had decreed that Jewish students could no longer attend public schools, and that those who had been enrolled were to be expelled. Likewise expelled from the schools "of every order and level" were the Jewish teachers, from the elementary schools to the universities.

No more Jews, in other words, contaminating the schools of the Kingdom of Italy.

At first, I didn't seem capable of understanding. That is, of course, I understood, the words were perfectly clear, but I couldn't seem to apply those formulations to myself. It would be forbidden for Jewish teachers and professors to go back to school, fine, but I caught myself thinking that this generic prohibition was aimed only at an abstract teacher, and not at the concrete person that I was, with my concrete plans and programs and my concrete personal way of understanding my relations with my students.

What the devil! Before the school year ended, I had even assigned my students an exercise, a piece of extended homework to do over the summer holidays. I wanted them to make a stab at translating the verse of Simonides of Ceos: not a literal translation but an attempt to turn it into a poem in the modern style.

They were very talented second year high school students (yes, I had taken the state exam and now I was a teacher at a classical high school), and I was pretty sure they'd do something remarkable with it. I would read their compositions in class, and together we'd select the best ones. That was the plan. I could hardly leave all their hard work without a fitting conclusion! Moreover, I had made a pledge to bring my students fully prepared to the admission exams for the third year of high school.

This is why I stubbornly persisted in my belief that the law was one thing and its practical application quite another.

"I don't think they'll let you go back to teach in your school," Sonia said to me, a little frightened when she realized that I was giving free rein to these vague and slightly unrealistic thoughts.

But I'd already made up my mind. I would go and talk to the principal of the school. In my conversation, I'd clear up all those problems that were holding me in a limbo, albeit still a hopeful one. After all, I was the best teacher at that school. You shouldn't think of me as conceited; it was an established fact and I was aware of it. Everyone at school agreed, including the principal—he had no great love for me, since politically I always remained subdued and neutral, but despite himself he had an annoyed respect.

And then I could please my father-in-law by taking a first stab at the qualifying examinations to teach at the university level, though up till now I had done nothing but postpone the moment. I realized that what I liked best about teaching was the ongoing relationship with young people, at an age when their minds were just opening up to the mystery of comprehension and understanding of the world. Thus, part of me continued to want to continue to teach high school.

And so that day I walked briskly toward my school, propelled by this awareness which served me as a brace, a support.

It was a beautiful day, the trolleys screeched past in satisfaction, the shops were still offering summer fruit, and everything seemed so normal. Why should I alone, for no good reason on earth, change all the essentials of my everyday life?

There was my school, with its oversized portal and the crumbling plaster.

As always, in the atrium I encountered the elderly custodian, who answered to the improbable name of Geronimo. He was a gentle man, whose personality hardly evoked that of his combative namesake; he was invariably easygoing and sunny, the way that large people often seem to be.

"Where do you think you are going?" he asked me this time, with a blend of embarrassment and hostility that really didn't suit him. And as he asked, he sort of shifted his substantial bulk to one side, to keep me from getting by him.

"Geronimo, I'd like to talk to the principal." I was looking at him with a relaxed and quizzical gaze, but he wouldn't meet my eyes.

"You wait here," he muttered furiously (perhaps he was furious with himself). "Because my orders are very clear . . . that is, I can't let in people . . . people like you."

A very short while later I saw him coming back; in spite of everything, he was disconsolate in his long fluttering grey smock.

"The principal said that if you need to get any of your things from the teachers' room, that I should accompany you."

I tried to insist, I explained again that I really needed to speak to the principal. My tone of voice was no longer quite so tranquil. And Geronimo blurted angrily, "Don't you see, he won't receive you, understood?" and then, his voice regaining a veneer of courtesy, he repeated the line about . . . "if I needed to get something."

Get something? In the locker that I pulled open absent-mindedly there were still two textbooks, marked and under-lined, and a pencil. I hardly knew what to do with that junk. The pencil was blunted, and the textbooks were from the second year of high school.

I automatically picked up the rather threadbare volumes. I didn't know what else to do.

Then I started toward the portal, with those ridiculous books under my arm, walking uncertainly, as if I were a student who had just been flunked at an exam.

Before walking out into the street and the open air, for some reason, I turned around, perhaps to say goodbye to old Gero-nimo, or maybe to bid farewell to the hallways of the school. All I saw, a little behind me, was the custodian in his tattered uni-form, raising one arm in a grotesque rendering of a Fascist salute.

This uncertain homage to the Fascist regime was all that remained to me of the place to which for so many years I had devoted myself heart and soul.

# CHAPTER SEVENTEEN

Y ou understand? The Community is putting together a number of Jewish schools . . . and apparently they intend to set up some high schools too." Ruben had clearly hurried over as soon as he heard about this new development, and he seemed pretty excited about it; I listened absently to him as he talked excitedly.

"This is good news," Ruben went on. "You wouldn't have to give up teaching."

"Why would the Community want to hire a bad Jew like me?" I answered after a long pause, as if I were talking to myself.

"What does being a 'bad Jew' have to do with it?" Ruben answered in a fury. "What our schools need are good teachers, and that's all that matters. The issue of training good Jews or not-so-good Jews is for the rabbis to worry about, not school-teachers."

Still, I kept warding off the idea, even though Sonia had joined forces with Ruben in trying to push me in that direction.

"I just don't feel up to it," I replied brusquely, "at least not this year." What I needed, before I could think of anything else, was a chance to gather my thoughts. You can imagine, I hadn't really fully absorbed what had happened . . . I certainly was in no condition to take up arms in a new battle as if nothing had happened, as if I hadn't just been unexpectedly demoted and demeaned.

Maybe for the next school year, who could say. But how

could I imagine that there wouldn't be a "next school year" for me?

It was only after I had put up this strenuous resistance (against who, after all?) that I remembered that Ruben was a person and I looked him in the face.

"What about you and your job?" I asked him at last, doing my best to put a little warmth into my voice.

"They'll keep me on at the law firm," Ruben replied in a faltering voice, "as long as I don't sign any legal documents with my own name, and as long as I don't make any court appearances."

"The invisible man, spinning his web in the shadows," I murmured under my breath, and Ruben retorted harshly: "Better to be invisible than nonexistent."

Then a little of the tension went out of his voice as he told me that his parents and other relatives of his who had stores more or less like Tutto per la sposa were making the same kind of arrangements. They were putting the permits in the names of trusted salesmen and longtime clerks, which often meant changing the terms of business—to the benefit of clerks and salesmen, of course. They did their best to stay out of the public eye and everything—with a few additional complications and inconveniences—went on just as before.

"If you can find a way around it, you can make things work"—this was the pragmatic approach that Ruben was explaining to me. Was this how we were expected to live, from now on?

I couldn't wait for Ruben to leave. I wanted to have some time alone and, most of all, I felt an urge to hurry to the Albergo della Magnolia. It was the one place that seemed unchanged, a haven of welcoming shadows, the magnolia that spread its branches to the fifth-floor windows, the hushed murmurs of the staff and the guests.

Now even the house in the Via Borgelli struck me as hostile and unsettling, with all those people constantly trying to start a conversation, and Sonia with her all-too-evident anxiety about me continually showing through.

Till now, my parents and I had talked in reasonably tranquil tones about the fact that I had been forced to leave my position at school. I had been reluctant to ask about the hotel, though. It seemed to me that in more intricate and specific matters like a private hotel, the new regulations were still unclear, and I certainly didn't want to add needlessly to any worries my mother and father might be feeling.

And in fact, as soon as my mother saw me that day, she asked if I would be teaching at the Jewish school, and I understood that Ruben must have spoken to her. I also thought to myself that I had been right: my mother made no mention of the hotel.

How wrong I was. When my father entered the room, I understood that once again I had been luxuriating in my usual ill-advised illusions.

How can I ever forget the words my father said to me that day? There my father stood, erect and elegant, poised with the customary imperturbable expression on his face, as he succinctly informed me that he had come to an understanding with Tiberio. "I'm putting the hotel permit in his name," he explained. "From now on, Tiberio is going to be the official manager of the Albergo della Magnolia."

Tiberio? Our devoted maître d'? Certainly, he was a reliable and intelligent worker, but he always walked respectfully in my father's wake, trailing him by more than a few steps. To think of putting the hotel in his name. Absurd.

"It is my impression that no specific regulations have been handed down concerning hotels and the like," I replied tersely, deeply offended at having been informed only after the fact.

My father failed to understand—maybe he was unwilling to understand. "Oh, there will be, you wait and see: they'll issue regulations," he replied in a neutral tone of voice, almost as if he were trying to reassure me in some odd manner. "In a few days the text of the law will be published and you'll see: everything we imagine will become explicit and official."

At this point, I felt incapable of asking my parents whether they would also be forced to move out of the private apartment, the little mansard apartment where I was born and raised.

My father explained matters to me without being asked. What he said more or less coincided with Ruben's view of things, that they would go on working behind the scenes, without showing their hand—in other words, concealing themselves behind Tiberio—and that therefore, for the time being, they could stay up there, in our little apartment tucked away above the fifth floor. In fact, it would be easier to take care of bureaucratic matters from the confinement of a little hideaway, and for that our apartment would be perfect.

I suddenly envisioned my father and mother perched like birds of the night on the highest branches of the tree, while far below tremors shook the earth and soil began sliding away in a gradual collapse.

And that was when my father informed me that he had decided, without undue haste, and taking as many months as was necessary, but before it was too late (yes, those were his exact words, "before it's too late," but he understood the world better than I did), to sell the hotel, perhaps even to Tiberio, who had said he might be interested.

I can't tell you the shock of pain that ran through me, as if someone had sent a bolt of electricity through my limbs. The Albergo della Magnolia was certain to vanish from my world . . . you see? I saw the one crag of solid land sink under the waves, the reef that my fingers had been clutching for as I swam desperately away from the wreckage.

You may scoff at the thoughts that had been running through my mind—unrealistic and ridiculous thoughts that they were.

When it dawned on me that I had lost my school, and my life as a teacher, I sought refuge in the idea that I could devote all my energies to running the hotel. I imagined how I would spend my days there, busy answering letters or discussing business matters with my father, perhaps even enjoying some leisure time, now that the urgent demands of my former profession no longer troubled me.

I had been confident that a private concern, a business that had nothing to do with the national government, public-private agencies, and the like, would be outside the interests of the Fasist regime. But I was mistaken. Once again, I had been foolishly naïve, but then and there it hadn't been easy to guess what it was that Mussolini really meant to do. Now of course we know, but it's easy to decipher the plan with the benefit of hindsight.

It wasn't merely an attempt to rid the state and its appendages from the influence of "untrustworthy" individuals: what lay in wait for us was the destruction of our way of life, of our very existence, the absolute and indiscriminate destruction of our world.

And that was how I finally lost the Albergo della Magnolia.

"The time has finally come for you to devote yourself to Pindar," Sonia started suggesting to me. "You've really neglected him over the past few years!"

Well, that was true. It had been months, it had been years since I had really sat down to take the intricate job of translating in hand. First there had been the plans for the wedding, then Michele had been born, then I had had to study for the qualifying exam for teaching high school. But Pindar was still there, waiting for me.

I hadn't forgotten him, I hadn't lost my eagerness to plunge into that enterprise, to devote myself heart and soul to that translation, that interpretation. In fact, deep down I cherished a secret joy, the knowledge that I possessed a hidden treasure, a trove tucked away in a grotto, and at the moment of my choosing, I could bring it glittering into the light of day.

Yes, at a moment of my choosing—but not now.

I couldn't use Pindar as a medication, as a cure-all to blunt the pain of a throbbing wound. If I had taken up Pindar at that juncture, I would have felt like one of those unhappy married couples who decide to have a child in an attempt—a vain attempt—to patch up a relationship tattered by continual misunderstandings and quarrels.

Pindar was a certainty that sprang from the most vital and vigorous forces of my creativity; he was not a penny to be flung at the feet of a pauper, starving or otherwise.

And so I spent my days doing nothing, absolutely nothing.

One day I took Michele to the zoo, and the following day I offered to take him to the park. The nanny, who was waiting at the front door, and Sonia too, both looked over at me in astonishment.

"Giulia and Maurizio are waiting for me at the park," Michele cried in excitement, "you can meet them; you can meet their nanny too . . . her name is Isa, I really like her."

Little boys, little girls, nannies, parks and playgrounds, what was my life turning into? To what freakish absurd pursuits would I turn to fill my days?

I began leaving the house, all by myself, to take long walks. All things considered, at least Ruben was still working, admittedly on a reduced scale.

"If you want, I'll come with you," Sonia said in a hesitant voice. But I knew what Sonia's days were made up of. Look, I wasn't judging her, not at all, that was just how the women of the Italian middle class lived back then. She had appointments with her girlfriends, with her dressmaker, her milliner, her hairdresser. Moreover, Sonia had volunteered at the Ada Negri, at the Casa del Fascio, to conduct a sort of afterschool tutoring session for the children of the poorer families. It was a good thing to do, light years away from the benefit balls and the card tournaments her mother organized, and I had encouraged her.

Was I ready to ask Sonia to give up her normal routine, her everyday life, for me? I couldn't ask that of her, and there was also the fact that—there was also the fact that I wanted to be on my own, to take long walks alone.

I wandered for miles, with no specific destination; sometimes I'd venture as far as the National Library, but I always stopped short and turned back, because I knew I wouldn't be allowed to enter.

One day I found myself, without even realizing how I got there, standing outside my old school when classes let out. I had stopped on the sidewalk across the street, just as I had that day outside the synagogue on Yom Kippur, when I ran into Ruben.

The students were leaving the building in small groups, or, in some cases, alone. They were normal children of that age: some were tall, others short, one was almost a grownup, another was still a child. Then I picked out the cluster of students from my class, with pretty Angela still wearing a ponytail.

They were already hurrying off, a few walking rapidly, others still chatting lazily and laughing. As always. For them, nothing had changed. Nothing had changed in the entire universe.

"Why don't you read books anymore?" Sonia pestered me, but I was angry at books. The world was full of books, stack them one atop the other and the pile would reach to the sky, but there were no books that could stop what was happening to us.

What good were books?

One evening I came home to find Gherardo. As usual, I arrived late, having spent the day roving restlessly. It was clear that Sonia had shared her worries about me with her cousin.

Gherardo started talking to me right away, accentuating his usual lighthearted banter with an exaggerated and contrived emphasis, as if we were meeting for the very first time and he were trying to make an impression.

He immediately launched a series of attacks on the race laws, with vivid and ferocious expressions, but I didn't find them amusing. I would have been more comfortable with a subdued tone, even a string of banalities, but something more in keeping with my mood and with the state of things.

After a while, Gherardo turned serious. Clearly, what he was saying now came from the heart.

"Listen," he explained, "for a genuine thinker it is an advantage not to have a full-time job. Actually, that's the natural state of an intellectual. Think about it carefully, none of the characters of the great novels of the eighteenth and nineteenth centuries have jobs. They don't have to do anything all day. They love, they suffer, they intrigue, they write letters, they travel, they return home. There is never a mention of any profession, of work, however monotonous. They all live on interest, on their own independent fortunes or else on debts that they sometimes fail to repay. But they never work. Work is a recent invention, it's not a natural pursuit for men, and certainly not for gentlemen. An intellectual lives in a world apart, made up of thought and culture . . . an entire lifetime would not be long enough to explore all the experiences that brim up inside him."

"It's come to this: talking about literature. Is that all we're allowed to do?" I replied grimly, irritated at his somewhat abstract tirade.

"You certainly won't starve; you've still got your income from the hotel, as well as Sonia's income," Gherardo said after a pause, as if he had read my mind (he seemed to do it often, as I've mentioned). "And so?" he went on, with renewed energy. "The world is full of books waiting to be read, museums to visit, antiquities to be rediscovered, music to listen to. These are the only things that truly matter, and they give life its real meaning. Why do you insist on this squalid desire to place your signature on a receipt for a paycheck?!"

"We're on the brink of a general breakdown, Europe is certainly moving toward another war, you can see for yourself what they're doing to the Jews in Italy and Germany, and you talk about books to read and museums to visit!" I shouted at him in exasperation. "All of this languid strolling through Arcadia is well and good if it's what you truly want to do, the result of one's free will, but not if it just turns into a way to stick your head in the sand, a way of turning a blind eye to what's happening in the world . . . and in our country!"

"Caro Dino, these are theorizations," Gherardo went on, by no means offended at the tone I had taken. "Beauty and art can fill your life with meaning, no matter the situation. I live for them, and I am perfectly happy."

I had serious doubts that Gherardo really was "perfectly happy." That is why I stopped arguing and, producing something resembling a smile for his benefit, I changed the subject.

# CHAPTER EIGHTEEN

You should not assume that in this troubled period Lorenza had dropped out of sight. I have mostly told you about myself and about other people (my parents, Ruben) who were, like me, involved in the headlong rush of events in that fatal year, 1938.

As I have told you more than once, Sonia remained close to me, but so did Lorenza.

From time to time, Lorenza, who knew about my obsession with long solitary walks, would happen by the house early in the morning and say to me: "I'm going to walk over to the university, why don't you accompany me," and so we would leave the house together, with a shared, and real, destination.

As we walked together, we would chat as we had in the past, but with an added patina of somberness. Lorenza too had moments of sadness and worry, as if her outlook had been stripped of all vigor, her thoughts seemed somehow to have been weighed down . . . in short, they no longer took flight the way they once had. It was even more striking when she'd suddenly turn remote and become lost in anguished thoughts that were not typical of her.

It struck me as hard to imagine that all this was because of her fond empathy for what had happened to me, a teacher, all things considered, of some considerable talent who no longer had anyone to listen to him.

Lorenza was fond of me, and I cared about her, but I was perfectly well aware that no one falls into a depression over someone else's troubles.

From time to time I'd try to change the subject to her, but Lorenza, as I explained to you before, had a guarded and reserved personality, and she defended her inner core with claws extended.

She had found some tutoring work for me. A girlfriend of hers had a sister who'd come down with pneumonia and had missed months of school, so she needed private lessons.

"You'll have to go to their house," Lorenza had explained quickly, "my friend's family won't let her go to strangers' houses."

So I'd have to go make home deliveries of my knowledge like a door-to-door salesman of learning? The idea struck me as so grotesquely punitive that I decided to accept.

To tell the truth, I actually enjoyed those private lessons; the girl I was tutoring was intelligent and eager to catch up, and her family refrained from asking me personal questions. They did, however, offer to pay me less than the going rate for my time.

I remember that I actually confided in Lorenza more than I did with Sonia, but that was only because I didn't want to add any new fears and worries to those that were already tormenting my wife so profoundly.

Perhaps losing the Albergo della Magnolia, I tried to explain to Lorenza, had caused me a pain that was even deeper and more blunt than being forced out of my teaching position. The Albergo della Magnolia had been the safe harbor of my childhood, the refuge in the enveloping half-light that muffled the noises from the outside world. When you were there, you were never alone, but you were never bothered by unwanted company either. That was one of the focal points of my life. In the other focal point, of course, were my practical and intellectual achievements and all that sort of thing.

Lorenza listened to these bemused meanderings in silence, then, with her customary reluctance to engage in conversations that might prove to be excessively revealing, she shifted the topic to more concrete matters. She told me, for example, that my parents had been overhasty when they transferred responsibility for the hotel, since the law concerning such specific cases (cases that, all things considered, were also pretty rare rare) had not yet been issued, and might never be.

Lorenza hadn't glimpsed the future very clearly. My father had.

At the end of November the decisions of the Grand Council of Fascism became the law of the state and they were deployed like a vast brightly colored fan, until they finally covered over the entire landscape of Jewish life in Italy.

In fact, among other things the law specified that Jews could not own buildings worth more than a certain amount; Jews were also forbidden to run companies.

Among the first few clauses of the law, moreover, was the decree prohibiting mixed marriages.

Mixed marriages were forbidden. I had known her for many years by now, but I can safely say that I had never seen Lorenza so overwrought.

At first I thought that she was so deeply upset because of what she had read in the text of the law, with its increasingly absurd articles and niggling regulations that prohibited, for example, the publication of Jewish names in phone books. And so I believed that it was all these things, and other such grotesqueries of the sort, that had smashed headlong into her optimism, however cautious it had been. But no, that couldn't be the only reason Lorenza was upset.

"They've prohibited mixed marriages," Lorenza suddenly said to us. "It means there's no future for us."

Who could she have meant by "us"? What did she mean by that phrase? Once again I sensed that I had been deaf, blind, obtuse. But Sonia too stared at her in wide-eyed astonishment. Why on earth had Lorenza chosen to shout at us, out of all the clauses of the law, that one, that particular detail? Why had she said in a dull monotone "there's no future for us"?

Then I began to see the light, making its way through a few initial doubts; I began to guess at the hidden meaning.

Lorenza and Ruben. How could I have missed it? Yes, it was true, they often went out together, and sometimes I had noticed them off to one side, taking intensely to one another, separate from everyone else, but I just assumed that they were both involved in various conspiratorial activities, that they had become, so to speak, "comrades in the struggle."

Once everything was clear to me, I remember that I felt a sharp stab of pain at how obtuse I'd been, at how I'd failed to understand them, how out of touch I'd been, despite the depth of my affection for them both.

Instead, perhaps, I had chosen to understand only a part of the truth.

Lorenza and Ruben, aside from the struggle against Fascism, loved one another and were planning a life together.

"You and Ruben?" I finally managed to murmur. "You and Ruben . . . why didn't the two of you tell us?"

"What need was there to tell anyone? If someone wanted to see it, they had eyes."

If someone wanted to see . . . and that was the point. Certainly Sonia, with all the hardships we had run into in our attempts to build a life together, could never have tolerated seeing the same thing unfold before her eyes, especially at such a starkly tragic time. A spectacle that, moreover, the family would absolutely have forbidden.

And that was why Sonia had kept her gaze downward, to keep from seeing.

And me? I was too occupied with my own problems and too fond of both Lorenza and Ruben as individuals to be able to think of them as a separate and self-contained couple. I would have immediately felt threatened by them as a couple, stripped of something that was profoundly and exclusively important to me.

I remember that day as a moment of pain that stabs me again every time that I open up the desk drawer of memories. Lorenza bursting into tears, for the first time in our presence, Ruben arriving a short while later, he, too, deeply shaken.

"Ruben, why didn't you tell us about the two of you?" I insisted, this time addressing him.

Ruben stared at me in astonishment. "What was there to tell you? It was all so clear . . . We were still making plans, and we hadn't yet figured out a path forward that we could tell our friends about."

This reply struck me as chilly and distant. He had referred to us generically as "friends," and suddenly that term struck me as so belittling, so inadequate to the feelings I had for Ruben and Lorenza.

From that day on, Ruben and Lorenza stopped seeing one another. Or at least they tried, but to tell the truth they were unsuccessful. I understood that when Lorenza happened to drop by our house and sat there, tense and still in her chair, obviously waiting for the sound of the doorbell.

Ruben sensed that and somehow always managed to guess the right moment to ring that doorbell. Sometimes they left together as they had in the old days, other times Ruben would say in a hesitant tone of voice, "Well, it's late . . ." and Lorenza would respond, "Ciao," lips clamped together, white from the pressure, seated immovable on her chair, staring blindly at the paintings on the wall.

At this point, I think I need to give you a little help in understanding the situation. Yes, because times were really different back then. For Lorenza and Ruben there really was no possible solution.

There were a few eccentrics who might perhaps think of

making a choice in favor of an anarchically free form of life, unfettered by any social restraint, perhaps some artists, or else professional revolutionaries, perhaps.

Lorenza was independent, rebellious, but always within the context of a bourgeois family life. Certainly, Lorenza—before the official passage of the law that lopped the head off any possibility of a mixed marriage, whatever form it took—in contrast with Sonia (there is no judgment in what I say here; it's a simple and straightforward statement of fact), would have been perfectly capable of breaking all ties with her parents, renouncing their approval and the considerable support they could offer, in order to marry Ruben in a simple civil ceremony.

For that matter, I had understood that was what they had planned, and I was deeply moved at the idea.

With that gesture, Lorenza would have shown that she was ready to repudiate the values or the non-values of her family in order to choose Ruben, that is, my world. That is, me.

Now however, in the face of a national law, making her the target of legalized persecution by the Fascist regime, and without the protection of any formal state of matrimony, not even someone as strong-minded as Lorenza would run that risk.

Nor would Ruben have ever asked her to do so. It would have been too radical a step, it would have meant becoming an outlaw, no longer a simple and silent opponent of the regime, as they now were with their hesitant anti-Fascism.

The word "impossible," which Lorenza would never have accepted from the Gentile family, now loomed over all of us from above, extending its reach over the entire territory of Italy.

That word had crushed Ruben and Lorenza, as it had done to so many others at the same time and for the same reasons. That's how these things happened. A tragedy becomes an even greater tragedy when life manages to strike down a winner, an inherently victorious soul.

# Chapter Nineteen

T he only advantage of the dark situation that had developed in those months was that I had stopped attending the family dinners in the Gentile home.

The hostility that Giuseppe Gentile felt toward me, reasonably well disguised over the years, occasionally behind a mask of what appeared to be an indulgent approval, had exploded in an unmistakable manner on the same day that the "Manifesto of Racist Scientists" was published.

I told you how that day he stormed unannounced into our house to say to me, in a threatening tone, and in the officially sanctioned *voi* form of address: "Now you see? I was right." The phrase was completely obscure in meaning, but in its violent irrationality it unveiled all too clearly his true and unflagging hostility toward me.

Even Sonia had been painfully forced to agree with me, and now when she went to see her parents she went, sadly, alone, or with Michele, but not as often as she had once done. She dropped by every so often, just enough to keep her family ties alive.

I had noticed in any case that the time she spent with her parents did Sonia little good, that every time she went to see them, she returned home saddened and grim. I even pointed it out to her.

It had never been my intention to separate her from her family, indeed, I had made every effort—and they were efforts!—since I had met her to allow her to be close to them, but now things were different. What was the purpose of it now, if seeing her parents only made Sonia feel worse instead of cheering her up?

When I talked to her about this, Sonia scarcely listened to me and raised no objections. I noticed however that sometimes she chewed nervously at her lip, a tic or habit that she had never displayed before.

One day I chanced to overhear, as I walked by the telephone, that the voice coming out of the earpiece was that of Sonia's father. Sonia sat listening in silence, replying every so often with a faint "*sì*," and then falling back into silence. After that phone call, she hurried out of the apartment.

One evening toward the end of the year, Sonia spoke to me.

Looking up at me with the anguished gaze that by now was customary with her, she told me in a small voice that that coming autumn Michele would be starting school. After a moment's silence, since I had nothing to say about a self-evident fact, she nervously added that at school Michele would be enrolling with a surname that appeared on the list of Jewish surnames. Even though he had been baptized, all his documents would list him as belonging to the "Jewish race" on his father's side. In short, Michele would be classified as "mixed." A "*meticcio*"—or half-breed—according to a newly published magazine.

"That's the way it is," I answered, and then, stupidly, I added, "I'm so sorry about it."

Sonia then went on to say that her father, with the help of Renato Martini and a few friends who were lawyers at the Sacred Roman Rota, or ecclesiastical court, had carefully studied the Nuremberg laws passed by the Nazis and the juridical status of the Jews in Germany.

The general impression they had all gathered was that the "mixed offspring" were considered as a separate category, but that from the information filtering back it seemed that in most cases this distinction was not actually taken into account. In fact, the hatred against the Jews was likely to overflow its banks, as we had so clearly seen during the recent *Kristallnacht*, or Night of Broken Glass . . .

Mussolini had drawn up his race laws on the model of the laws of the Third Reich . . . In other words, Sonia cringed as she expressed the thought, the same things might happen here in Italy . . .

"I don't know what might become of our son one day!" Sonia finally said, bursting into tears.

"What can I do about it!" I shouted in exasperation. "Even if I disappeared, ran away somewhere, or killed myself, my surname and his 'mixed birth' would still be there!"

"There might be a way to re-register his paternity," Sonia said to me, practically in a whisper.

I stopped and stared at her. That wasn't a phrase that had come out of the blue, in a sudden access of frustration. No, here was a specific idea. But that behind it there might be a well-thought out plan, well, that was something I would never have imagined.

"And how do you re-register a child's paternity? Tell me more," I ventured, just for the sake of something to say.

"You'd have to modify some documents, you'd have to falsify a few things, and of course you'd need the cooperation of certain authorities who can help us."

"Explain exactly what you're talking about," I said, this time forcefully.

And Sonia explained everything.

She suffered as she explained it, she tormented herself over it the whole time, but despite everything, the details were pretty clear.

A disavowal of paternity, that's what she was talking about. Yes, a disavowal of paternity with a solid justification to buttress it. For instance, the Italian legal terminology was *impotentia generandi*, or infertility.

"My father is in touch with the right doctors and lawyers. It's just a question of money."

Her father . . . then it was all true. Those people had prepared a plan, or rather, *the* plan. They had been huddled in secret concert, plotting around a table, for who could say how many days, scheming to reshape the destinies of others to suit their own purposes. They were the real "Elders of Zion."

It was too difficult for me to enter suddenly into the mindset of the *plan* and to follow its various phases with a normal capacity for rational thought. No, here, simple reason was insufficient.

"And so I would no longer be Michele's father, and Michele would be out of danger, an Aryan, one hundred percent, and the son of who knows who . . . right?" I murmured, and Sonia nodded her head.

"And . . . and our marriage?"

"Well . . ." Sonia twisted her hands spasmodically, "given the reasons, the Sacred Rota will annul it . . . but that would be a mere formality. Between us and deep within, nothing would change. We could still see one another and love one another just like before, I swear it . . . I don't understand how these horrible things can happen in this day and age, but they've happened, and there is nothing we can do . . . This too will pass, I know it, and one day everything will go back to normal. When the dark wave has exhausted its force and peace returns, it will all turn right again . . . I feel sure of it because . . . because they can change the way things are, but not the way we feel, if the feelings are as strong as they are with us."

"Sure, of course," I replied mechanically, because my mind couldn't follow the thread of this possibility.

The *plan*, they had developed and fine-tuned the *plan*, and Sonia was its mouthpiece. Its healthy carrier.

Yes, Sonia loved me, of that I was certain, just as I was sure that she wanted to go on seeing me, to preserve her relationship with me . . . of course, in that she was going against her father's wishes, but what did that matter . . . It was hardly her fault if she wasn't strong enough to withstand the blows of history.

But the only thing I cared about was making sure Michele was safe. Or, perhaps I should say, the thing I cared about *most*. If I was no longer responsible for my son, and therefore no longer responsible for Sonia either, I would feel lighter, freed of a burden, and able to decide about matters that would now concern only me. Or even to make no decision at all. The important thing was to be able to acquire that lightness. The important thing was to save my son.

The *plan* was not limited to a straightforward announcement. All the details were complicated, and they fit together in a long chain of interlocking steps, and each of them was essential, the chain could not be broken at any point. Meetings, examinations, documents, trips, and much, much more . . . everything had to be done carefully to complete the *plan*.

Once everything was complete, I knew perfectly well that I would be required at a certain point to go far away, and only later could I return to resume my life with Sonia, though now it would be as her secret lover. In fact, we would have to be even more careful than illicit lovers, because if we were caught together the whole paper castle of the annulment could collapse as a result.

But this wasn't the time to worry about the aftermath, an aftermath of details that I didn't want to consider just then. Now what was most important was deciding on the central issue. And concerning that central point, as I have already told you, I had been certain from the very outset.

The next day (or perhaps a lifetime went by) Lorenza arrived, Ruben arrived, and both of them begged me "not to do it," and they both attacked Sonia.

And Sonia changed her mind and she would say, heartbroken:

"They're right, let's forget about all this and entrust our fate to destiny," but then I realized that, when she was alone, she'd rethink it, and the primordial instinct to rescue her son would always win out. Then Sonia would hurry to embrace me, and she'd say, "We'll love each other forever," but I understood that when she hurried to my side, it was because the *plan* had wormed its way into her, along with the temptation to embrace the *plan*.

Often we wept and suffered together, but it was all pointless. As far as I was concerned, I had already decided. It seemed to me that it was my duty to my son.

Michele, you mustn't judge me for what I did. I did it out of love, I did it for your sake. And I never regretted having done it. It wasn't a kind of weakness, like my weakness in accepting everything in the conversation with your grandfather, even humiliation, in order to be allowed to marry Sonia, your mother.

This time I felt strong in the decision I had made. I wasn't "swept along" by others, finally it was me choosing and acting.

And I was right in my choice. Now we know how history turned out. Fathers in the ghettoes who hid their children in closets, concealing them beneath secret manholes, or throwing them in haste into the arms of strangers, or letting them slide off the running board of a freight train. Everything that could be imagined or that couldn't be imagined was done to save our children.

Sonia had been right as well. Often the "mixed" children did not survive. We have read and heard the stories of children hunted down, in some cases taken alone, where the parents had hidden them, and transported to concentration camps to be murdered or even subjected to the so-called medical experimentation.

I have no desire to lay before you the cavalcade of horrors. In some way, each of us has already learned and suffered on our own.

And me? Wouldn't I have locked you in a closet or nailed you into an attic hiding place, wouldn't I have thrown myself over you to serve as a human shield with my body, to protect you from a burst of machine-gun fire?

And instead, what did I do for you? I merely signed a series of horrible false documents and . . . I went on loving you.

# CHAPTER TWENTY

U nderstand me, Michele, I just couldn't do it. I was unable to adhere fully to the decision I had made. I wanted to lay before you an account of what had happened, an account that was objective, neutral, as far as I was able. A story in which I moved the characters back and forth as if they were just that—characters and nothing more—not, in various ways, a part of me. And of you.

As long as they were members of the family, I was able to carry out this operation, which corresponded to a deep-seated need of mine.

But as soon as we came to the crux of the story, the scorching moment in which a father felt he had been condemned by mankind at large to be stripped of his fatherhood, the dam broke.

Michele. That Michele is you.

I can't bring myself to speak of you in the third person anymore. Now I need to talk to you as directly and personally as possible, now that the dam has broken.

I will continue to present the others to you as "third persons," to keep from distorting too greatly the meaning of this operation that I am struggling to complete.

As you must have imagined, this torturous situation was a succession of highs and lows for both of us. Outside, however, where the *plan* was being developed and refined—albeit amidst countless obstacles—matters were moving forward along a precise and carefully planned-out line.

I still don't know why it took me so long to ask the question. It was a simple but fundamental point. Who, after all, would lend his name, who would lend himself, to act as your official father?

"We'll look for someone," Sonia said to me at the beginning, and she had explained to me that it would have to be someone who was completely reliable, ideally someone who lived in another city, to prevent chance meetings and potential interference. In turn, but in the interest of one and all, this hitherto imaginary person would be reassured and protected by a series of documents drawn up by lawyers and deposited with a notary, releasing him from all manner of obligations.

"And he must also be ready and willing," Sonia never failed to point out, with a pathetic insistence on this point, "he must be willing and ready to reverse matters, to undo what we've done when this general wave of madness has finally subsided, in some future time in which we can all go back to what we once were."

My mind was so bound up with doubts and problems that the question of this remote front man had been only a minor issue at the back of my mind, perhaps because the race laws had already led to a flourishing subindustry of fronts or straw men for all sorts of different situations. As a result the term had become part of everyday parlance.

One evening Sonia sat down next to me and with an exaggeratedly nonchalant manner told me that, in short, she and her family had already spent so much time thinking about this point and that, in the end, they had decided to fall back on the simplest solution. It really was silly that they hadn't thought of it before.

"Exactly what is this 'simple solution'?" I asked, without even a glimmer of the truth.

"Gherardo," Sonia answered in a tiny voice.

Gherardo? What on earth did Gherardo, the witty and footloose traveler, have to do with this grim little story of ours?

"Think about it." Sonia, now that she had broken the ice, had become more confident. "With Gherardo we'd have absolutely nothing to worry about. Someone like him would cause no trouble, and he'd never dream of trying to lay claim to anything . . . and with Gherardo a lot of things would fit together very conveniently."

"For instance?"

"For instance, Gherardo came to visit me when I was in Salsomaggiore, exactly nine months before Michele was born . . . You know, we can't just do things at random, and this particular 'reconstruction' would support the case we have to present. It has to be plausible . . . we need to think about how our story appears to third parties, and the detail of Gherardo gives the whole thing a degree of realism, the fact that he was in Salsomaggiore in that period can be documented."

"But . . . but that's monstrous!" I said, as if to myself, and suddenly I thought back to the impassioned letters that Sonia had written me from that spa, and the stories she'd told me about her cousin's visit . . . Yes, Gherardo, as was his way, with his unfailing and impeccably orchestrated seductiveness, had enchanted throngs of young wives as they intently sipped their lemonades and listened to the notes of Mascagni's "Iris" . . . I remembered very clearly that, among other things, Gherardo had scorned to stop at Sonia's hotel, charming and elegant though it was, and had hurried over to his usual stopping place, the Grand Hotel . . . But what did all this matter . . . and where had Gherardo actually slept? Was I slipping unwarily into the logical toils of the *plan*? And, after all, what better and more respected front could we hope for than a cousin with such titles of nobility?

Certainly, a deluxe front of this sort wasn't the sort of thing just anybody could obtain. Still, the idea continued to sound dark, and for some reason, even incestuous to me. I just couldn't help it.

As we know, you can't just give in to the first impulse that seizes you. I tried to force myself to be reasonable, and I had to admit as I thought it through that it was after all a sound idea to choose Gherardo, and then . . . and then, if one day it really happened (I was counting on it, Sonia wasn't alone in this) that the madness that was gripping the world finally quieted down, Gherardo—with his sardonic smile—would step aside in a flash.

"He even has the same last name," Sonia ventured timidly, having noted a change in my expression. "Michele could call himself Gentile, just like me. That way, it would be as if I had never shared him, even as a sham, with anyone other than you."

"What about Gherardo—is he willing?" I asked in my new guise as a reasonable interlocutor.

"He will only accept after he talks to you. You know how greatly Gherardo values your opinion. He would never agree to do something that might strike you as unfriendly."

And now that she had my full and undivided attention, Sonia hastily informed me that Gherardo would be coming to see me the following day. "He's already in Rome," she informed me.

Of course he was already in Rome; he had been summoned by the masterminds as they stealthily wove their *plan*.

That day may have been the first time that I saw Gherardo looking upset, less than perfectly in control of himself, and in any case in no mood to launch any of his sarcastic wit.

"How are we doing, old man?" he said to me, with an embarrassed half smile. For a moment, he tried to resume his old personality, drawing on at least a bit of his customary ferocity.

"You see what happened, just because you were so determined to become part of an Aryan family?"

He'd done his best, but his voice was a little flat, a bit lifeless.

"It's true, you tried to warn me . . . the very first night we met," I answered in the same tone of voice.

"I'll bet that the horseman and horsewoman, your two ineffable in-laws, haven't been around much."

"You'd win that bet."

It was pointless to keep delaying the inevitable, veering away from the topic that both of us cared about most. It wasn't easy, neither of us knew how to begin, but this was why Gherardo was here.

"Gherardo, let's talk it over," I said quietly, reaching out to lay my hand upon his.

I realized that the gesture had overwhelmed him.

"Dino! I don't know what I should do!" Gherardo was speaking with a note of despair in his voice; he seemed on the verge of losing control. "I swear to you, I would never, never let anyone talk me into doing anything that you might see as hostile . . . or that could be turned against you."

"I'm the one that wants this," I said clearly and calmly in a somber voice.

"Yes, that's what they told me, but I wanted to hear it directly from you . . . And really I don't understand you. I don't see why or who you are trying to please by willingly carrying out this masochistic act."

I did my best to explain my reasoning, I may even have used the same words that I used with Sonia, that I had used with Lorenza and Ruben, the same words that I wrote to you.

Gherardo appeared to be touched, but not entirely convinced.

"Literature, literature, it's a weakness of yours: you always think real life is just like literature . . . Mad love . . . charging in without looking, throwing caution to the winds, just like a Don Quixote, desperately trying to make life into a some kind of a dream . . . Wake up! Those days are gone forever . . . this is the real world, and it's a harsh, cruel world . . . Take your wife and your son, and run away somewhere . . . That, at least, wouldn't be literature!"

"Run where?" I replied wearily. "Or haven't you noticed that all Europe is exploding into war? Has it not occurred to you that step by step Hitler is going to devour us all? And then . . . Sonia . . . You were the one who described her as 'the pearl and the oyster,' you told me that I had to take the one with the other. Can you imagine Sonia uprooted from her family, a refugee, a bag thrown over her shoulder, wandering the roads of the world?"

"No, I can't imagine her doing that. But I can't see how they're going to pull off this huge machination, with you as the sacrificial lamb."

"Oh, they'll pull it off, don't you worry about that. They're masters of deceit and experts at pulling off frauds. The more complicated they are, the better they like them.

"Do you see?" I said, and I realized that I had changed my tone of voice, and now I was speaking to Gherardo with growing warmth. "You understand that I can accept this thing only from you, not from anyone else? From you, a man who is capable of looking at life with a clear-eyed, critical judgment, a friend, someone with whom I share a deep understanding."

For the second time that day, Gherardo seemed to be deeply moved.

"Well, if you want this, then I cannot say that I am opposed." Then he recovered and tried to resume the tone that suited him best. "And after all, maybe one day your son will inherit a sizable estate, that is, unless my mother really does disinherit me. She threatens to do it every other day, I'd say."

"You'll give him back to me with an inheritance," I tried to work up a smile.

"Your son is a good kid, he's not like those obnoxious nasty twins that the lovely Clotilde is bringing up . . . and in any case, he would be my sole and absolute heir . . ."

That was how the tension was finally broken. At last we had said what we needed to say, and now we could speak freely, like in the old days. It was in this new and confidential atmosphere that Gherardo committed an unforgivable misstep.

We were sitting there, chatting comfortably, as I said, allowing ourselves to indulge in random thoughts and vague emotions, when Gherardo felt the impulse to tell me something very personal.

"I have to admit something," he murmured, almost as if he were speaking to himself. "I know that it's only a masquerade . . . but there are times . . . I couldn't even say why . . . well, I feel a certain thrill when I tell myself that now I have a son . . . I know, it's only invented, it's just playacting, but I can't help it. After all, we're all just a stitched-together quilt of contradictions . . ."

Gherardo was speaking quietly, intently, and he failed to notice—he couldn't have noticed—what was happening inside me. An uncontrollable fury was surging up within me, blinding me, throttling me.

My son! He was talking about my son! Gherardo, the front, a hypothetical, abstract figure, was describing *to me* his fake emotions about his fabricated fatherhood.

He was taking my son and transferring something of his own into him, planting inside my son his intricate and ambiguous personality, where it could flower and take root.

I still don't know how I managed to master my rage, how I managed to conquer my overwhelming urge to stand up and seize him by the throat. But I did. Gherardo didn't deserve that. My rage was aimed at someone else. Even if I had explained it to him, he would have been baffled. He wouldn't have understand what a huge mistake he had made by choosing me as the confidante of his stolen love. Love he had stolen from me.

I managed to work up a pallid smile; Gherardo understood that our conversation had worn me out, and he left.

# CHAPTER TWENTY-ONE

T hen one day, when Sonia told me in a hesitant and profoundly saddened voice that the time had come for me
to look for another place to live, I finally made up my
mind to go and talk to my parents.

I had dawdled and perhaps left it too late, and for some time
now I had been tormented by a terrible fear that they might
have heard rumors, even if Ruben had promised (and certainly
maintained) absolute silence on the matter.

I admit that I was very good with them. What mattered
most—I secretly hoped—was not so much the words as the
tone of voice. Well, the tone of voice that I managed to use
when I spoke to them was as considered and neutral as possible,
as if I were telling them about an unexpected benefit conferred
by the world of the bureaucrats, the unlooked-for but positive
outcome of some complicated case or proceeding.

I told them in a tranquil tone of voice that, thanks to the
usual network of highly placed connections that my in-laws
enjoyed, as well as the payment of a substantial sum of money
to the father of a powerful member of the Fascist party, we had
managed to "Aryanize" Michele. And so, I told them, we could
look forward to Michele's upcoming years in school being free
from obstacles, and we could hope that this would prevent any
unpleasant incidents.

It was immediately clear to me that, in spite of everything
else, this piece of news would actually come as a relief to my
mother and father. And that's how it went.

It was only afterward that they asked me: "How did you manage it?" And it was only later that I explained, maintaining the same neutral tone of voice, that they had transferred Michele's paternity to a front, a willing stooge who had promised never to bother anyone.

In other words, the truth was coming out in small batches, and I did my best at each step to minimize the scope of the thing. It was true. Taken separately, each act seemed like a trifle. As long as you kept from putting them all together, as long as you refrained from looking at the plan as a whole.

I knew, though, that it wouldn't be long. I could see that my father was starting to add up the figures, and soon he'd have the final sum, he'd see the inevitable result.

In the end, I was forced to admit to him that I would move out "for a little while." At those words, I saw my father plunge into a state of gloom. Then I sensed that he was about to speak to me, about to say "Come back and stay with us," but that he had dropped the idea. Perhaps it was because I had just told him that Sonia and I would continue to see one another, though in a more or less clandestine manner.

My mother, too, after a quick glance over at her husband, seemed suddenly bewildered and lost. After a long silence, she asked me, "You won't bring Michele to see us anymore?" I reassured her that of course she would still see Michele, perhaps a little less frequently . . . and perhaps . . . they should take care not to insist on their status as "grandparents."

I hated myself afterwards for having specified that detail. Deep down I knew that they would never, or only very rarely, be able to see their "no-longer grandson."

It was going to be hard for me too . . . But the *plan* couldn't take feelings into account . . .

Sonia found me a place to live; it was in the same neighborhood, so that it would be easier for us to meet. For me to see her and see you, Michele.

The address was symbolically located along a line running between the Via Borgelli and the Albergo della Magnolia, though it was a little closer to the hotel. That suited me, because I went to see the Albergo della Magnolia (though without going in, because I didn't want to reveal my weakness) practically every day. I would wander past the place, absorbed in thought, and then walk briskly away . . .

The place that Sonia had taken for me was very nice. It was a three-room apartment on the ground floor of a pleasant Art Nouveau building that stood along one of the countless little tree-lined streets of the neighborhood: French doors opened onto a combination garden-courtyard in the rear, with a few trees (no magnolia, though) and a flowerbed bounded by sharp stones.

Sonia had made sure that there was a small magnolia tree in a vase, though, in a prominent location, on the coffee table next to the sofa in my new living room.

I have to say that Sonia made sure that the apartment was furnished, nicely decorated, and filled with everything I would need, while I looked on in bewilderment, unable to understand what she was doing.

She had even found me a housekeeper, who fortunately went back to her own home after making me dinner.

Once I managed to take mental possession of this strange new life of mine, I asked her to set the table at four in the afternoon and then leave.

Some days I made the excuse that I would be traveling, and I would tell her not to come at all. But I never let Sonia know when I did that.

That same March day in 1939, the day that Hitler's army invaded the part of Czechoslovakia that he hadn't seized six months earlier, and the thudding footsteps of his warriors echoed funereally through the streets of Prague, I found myself once again as a spectator in a grotesque ritual that had to do with some church or other.

In this new ritual, it was proclaimed that my marriage with Sonia had never existed, or, that even if it had existed, it had been nothing more than a farce, a fiction.

While I stood there, wandering over distant terrain in my mind, I thought of another, very different day, in the chapel where my Pauline marriage rites were held, when I had been the passive protagonist of a different ceremony, in a very different frame of mind. Yes, I had been a spectator then as well, but I was a spectator fully involved in Sonia's most profound emotions.

I'll never forget how deeply moved Sonia had been. It gave meaning to everything I was doing. Now . . .

Now I had to take the most painful step, the only thing that really made me want to run away, to disappear, to be catapulted suddenly and magically to the ends of the earth.

Now I had to tell you about it, Michele.

I imagine you have no memory of that conversation. Or, if you do, I doubt you remember the words that were spoken, nor how you moved, how I watched you, and the way that Sonia looked at you. In your mind, there may be some vague, indistinct recollection of something troubling. For me, it was a laceration, a wound that never healed. Never will, as long as I live.

I would tell you that Sonia was really very good at it—if it weren't that the word sounds grotesque and almost obscene, referring as it does to something that was bound to ravage many lives and many worlds.

Sonia explained to you, more or less, as I recall, that if you love someone, that's what matters most . . . whether that person is your father . . . or uncle . . . or cousin, that's not so important. What's important is that you love them. She told you that I loved you and I was happy that I could spend time with you, but that I wasn't your real father. Then who was I? Well, I was a distant uncle.

And now we would go on seeing one another and loving one another just like before, but I wouldn't be able to live with you anymore. It was better for me to live on my own, in another house, especially because I needed long periods of silence so that I could write a very hard, very complicated book.

"But I promise to be quiet!" you answered, Michele, looking at me with bewilderment in your eyes, "I'll let you work in peace . . . If you want, I'll turn the pages of the books with the ants for you."

How can I express to you how hard and deep that hit me? How can I describe the feeling, as my very being flew apart in a thousand scattered shards, as if it had been blown apart by an explosion? How can I recount what I tried to tell you that day, words and words that came out of my mouth, the words that I quoted to you just a moment ago, words I hope you can't remember, and other words that I hope you do remember.

And I explained again that it wasn't so important to live together, all that mattered was that we could go on seeing one another, talking together, telling each other everything, the way we always had. And you listened to me, wordlessly.

Michele, you dearly loved my wristwatch, and whenever we sat next to one another, you did your best to unbuckle it and slip it off my wrist; you could never quite get it off because I kept you from doing so. It was the game we played.

This time, I unbuckled it and slid it off my wrist; I gave it to you, without you even asking.

So now there you were, intently focused on the workings of that wristwatch; you were even twisting the little knob on the side, sweeping the minute and hour hands back and forth; something that you remembered perfectly well I had never allowed you to do before. But what did that matter now, in this strange new planet on which we had just landed?

You focused on that wristwatch for a long time, head bowed, twisting the little wheel tirelessly, spinning the hands up and down. It really seemed as if you weren't going to speak.

Then, all of a sudden, you asked, without looking up, as if you were asking the wristwatch this question: "Then who is my real father supposed to be?"

"It's Cousin Gherardo," Sonia answered immediately, using the term "cousin" that had made me smile the first time I heard them talk that way in their family.

"Cousin Gherardo?" You seemed even more bewildered. "Is he going to come live with us?" you asked after a moment of silence.

"Of course not! You know how Cousin Gherardo likes to travel, he has apartments and houses in places all around the world! And he's always so busy, he has to supervise the peasants as they work in the fields. You know, lots of people work for him, and he has to tell them all what to do.

"If you like," Sonia ventured, "sometime when they're harvesting grapes to make wine we could go watch . . . it's a lot of fun."

"I don't like grapes," you muttered, examining the watch, holding it close to your ear.

For a long time you said nothing more, intently busy with the wristwatch, then, after a silence that seemed to both of us to stretch out into eternity, you finally looked up.

"Who'll take me to the zoo?" you asked with a calm curiosity.

# CHAPTER TWENTY-TWO

S onia almost always came to see me in the evening. "It's so the concierge won't see me," she said, but I felt sure that it was really because she was terrified her father or some other member of her family might find out.

For that matter, on the first day Sonia had introduced herself to the concierge as my cousin (our time together was just one cousin after another; had you noticed?) and as a cover story it was very plausible, since Sonia had supervised the move, the furnishing of the apartment, and an endless array of other niggling matters.

Now, whenever she dropped by for a brief stay during the day, in order to reinforce her role as a "helper in practical matters," Sonia would always make sure that the concierge saw her carrying packages or bundles, whether it was newspapers, tins of orange marmalade, or bottles of wine from Gherardo's estate, the Tenuta Castel Murmuzio.

So Sonia had transformed herself into a conspirator who arrived to nourish and provide sustenance to the great recluse, the prisoner in the grotto.

Aside from her, who ventured to come see me in my new home? Sometimes Ruben, but after he realized that Sonia might come by once darkness fell, he retreated. It wasn't the same as in the past. It certainly wasn't comfortable anymore for the three of us to sit around chatting.

Nowadays Ruben had a very clear impression that his presence only stole moments from us, chipping away even more at a vandalized relationship between a pair of lost spouses.

And so Ruben and I would meet occasionally in the street, and we'd trudge back and forth rehearsing our tired ideas, but by now inevitably in that grim new mood in which we barely managed to stave off despair.

Lorenza never came to see me—just once or twice with Sonia to see the apartment.

Still, you have to understand, the conventions of the era (and perhaps even the customs of later times) would have considered it awkward for a single woman like Lorenza to be alone in the apartment of a single man. I sometimes bumped into Lorenza, just as I did Ruben, on the street or in a café, but not often.

Aside from those chance meetings, I was alone.

I had doubled and, in time, tripled my private tutoring sessions; it seemed that word spread rapidly about this out-of-work professor—so learned, such a good teacher, so cheap! And that was all that was left to me.

I had not yet forgiven books for the way they'd betrayed me. I made an exception for murder mysteries: they at least seemed not to have taken part in the conspiracy. I had become a specialist in Agatha Christie and I was seized by a true obsession: I wanted to have a complete collection of her works. I spent hours picking over used-book stalls and junk stores, doing my best to find rare editions or out-of-print copies.

My only real connection to life, besides Sonia, was you, Michele. By now, I only ever saw you in the out-of-the-way tea shop where we went to have a cup of hot chocolate with whipped cream. I asked you questions, and sometimes you answered; other times you remained silent.

At first, it was all one unbroken experience, one flooding emotion for me to see Sonia standing before me, for us to wrap our arms around one another, embracing spasmodically for long minutes, and then move over to the window or the sofa, still embracing.

In those moments, life began coursing through me again, and begin to take on a semblance of meaning. But then . . .

Then time passed. With a growing feeling of alarm, I realized that this meaning was fading away, dissolving into a bubble made of nothing. The passionate gestures of the first few days were being transformed into a sort of ritual, rehearsed self-consciously by both of us.

Sonia would walk into the apartment with her fixed smile, plastered to her mouth like a decoration of some sort, and immediately did her best to draw me out in conversation, with overdone vivaciousness. Conversation about what, though? I wasn't working, and the only thing that filled my days was hunting for mysteries in the used-book stalls.

And who could we talk about? I never saw anybody . . .

So she tried to tell me something of her own life, which was, all things considered, fairly monotonous. Then she'd tell me about you, Michele, reporting the words you spoke, the things you did, the moods and feelings you revealed or concealed, and then, without a doubt, I listened closely, and with a sense of heartbreak.

After a while, though, this subject too ran out. We couldn't go on racking our brains over what you might be feeling deep down in that muddled situation that we had created for you. Before long, we were repeating ourselves.

Sonia knew that I never wanted to hear the names of her family members again. Father, mother, sisters, and spoiled little nephews were no longer part of my landscape. Luckily. But Sonia's everyday life was interwoven with their lives. Without those habitual points of reference, she lost most of her subjects of conversation.

What was left to us? There wasn't much of a choice. We still had sex.

But, oddly enough, that was where my crisis became most acute.

Michele. I am being merciless, I know; I'm telling you everything about me. I asked myself, before moving forward, whether it was right to descend into details of such an intimate and personal nature, when writing to a son. After all, we both know perfectly well that I'm talking about your mother.

If you were still a boy, of course, I would certainly have left out this entire part of my story. But you're a man now, capable of understanding and seeing matters with the necessary distance. I assure you that my focus on these details, touching them in passing, is not gratuitous.

No, it's important, and I hope that if you read through to the end you will understand why.

Sonia sensed that she was losing ground, that our relationship had wandered out onto quicksand, and so she grasped stubbornly at the only form of concrete bond that remained to us.

And the more firmly she grasped at that bond, the more daring and bold she became, the more I felt an instinct—an instinct that took me by surprise—to draw back, to flee from her.

I didn't like this Sonia, disheveled and in the grip of some fury, miming gestures that were alien to her. There was something off key in these new throes of passion, a passion that seemed to be shouted out more than experienced. I felt that the waves of instinctive and secret impulses were no longer flowing within her in the eternal currents of time, but were instead being guided into artificial, intentional channels.

I was used to a different Sonia. A Sonia who yielded, who became pliant within the boundaries of an age-old game of love in which I pushed and she allowed herself to be won, though in reality by yielding it was she who triumphed.

I don't want you to misunderstand me at this point. Don't

think of me as a conventional hidebound male, comfortable only with the time-honored role of dominator. No, I sincerely doubt that I've ever been that way. And if it had been natural from the very beginning for Sonia to behave sexually in that bold and aggressive manner, I would have been perfectly happy with it. But that's not how she was.

I was beginning to sense that this exasperated form of sex on Sonia's part sprang out of desperation, not out of passion. It was a piece of playacting. Unconscious, I feel sure, but still, rehearsed, playacted. Once again, we found ourselves plunging into a world of fiction, just as every other aspect of my life had turned into fictional props.

Fake, fake, fake, everything was fake, paternity, life, now even love was fake. Could it be that there was nothing left in my world that was authentic?

When Sonia left the apartment after our encounters, closing the door behind her, I was seized with a dull and ferocious sense of resentment. I imagined Sonia in her new guise as a second-class courtesan, I imagined her acting and lying. Lying to me, lying to the whole world.

And after all, who could say if the story of Gherardo really was entirely invented? How skillful they were, "the master-minds," at manipulating things, muddying the waters, and arranging for everything to wind up part of "their" network, "their" world.

And me, stupid me, tumbling naively into the trap, believing it all.

Just what had Gherardo really been doing in Salsomaggiore? Yes, he went to visit his cousin—actually, his cousin's daughter—to enliven his monotonous days of idleness. That wasn't really a very substantial motivation. Who could actually believe it?

And let's face it, Gherardo had always been an admirer of Sonia. Gherardo was an aesthete, and Sonia gratified his sense of beauty, and never undermined her loveliness with stupidity, the way her sister Clotilde did.

Of course, in that family there wasn't a single person who wasn't busy scheming, plotting to harm me.

Who cared! Let them plot! What did it matter to me anymore?!

What the devil, let Sonia slip into bed with her cousin, with someone who, after all, had the same surname, that is, if Gherardo liked that sort of thing!

Deep down inside, really deep down, I knew that even these nocturnal musings were fake, a comedy of cruelty that I inflicted on myself to torment myself and to torment Sonia.

How ridiculous, the very idea that Sonia, a newlywed, and Gherardo, in Salsomaggiore . . .

But . . . but, then why, just for the sake of an example, did Sonia suggest to you, Michele, that you go together to the countryside, to see the grape harvest on Gherardo's estate? What possible reason was there to come up with this idea of an outing, if Sonia had assured me that Gherardo's paternity would be merely virtual, and that her cousin would never interfere in the life of my son?

"Why did you tell Michele that you'd take him to see Gherardo?"

One evening I caught her off guard with this accusation, and Sonia turned pale. Really, at first she had no idea what I was talking about, because I had cunningly left out the detail of the grape harvest.

And while Sonia awkwardly tried to give me a simple explanation, saying that she had said it to give our conversation with you some semblance of normality, I pressed my attack, scolding her angrily for failing to respect our agreement that there would never be any contact between you and Gherardo.

Sonia's mistake had been to try to justify herself; she should have just shrugged and turned away. By trying to minimize, she had wandered unwarily onto my territory, and at the moment that meant walking into a veritable minefield. Now Sonia opted for silence, but she was too late.

Now I was pelting her with a hail of questions about Salsomaggiore. What did she and Gherardo talk about at Salsomaggiore? And where did they go for meals? Did they go alone or did they have company? How had they spent those three days? How did they while away the hours?

Sonia looked at me, astonished and appalled; she was speechless. The longer she remained silent, the more suspicious I became, until inside me my absurd hypothesis began to seem plausible.

Finally, Sonia burst into tears and I slowly began to repent.

How could I have staged such a cruel game? What was becoming of me? Who was I trying to take down with me in my plummeting descent? Sonia, whom I had loved and desired with such relentless tenacity? Sonia, who had returned my love with unexpected impetus despite the hardships arrayed against us, and who was now battling with her limited resources to keep from losing me?

I was overwhelmed by a profound and loving pity. I spent the rest of the night trying to persuade her to forgive me.

Occasionally, very rarely, we went to a movie, always to the same movie house on the outskirts of Rome, because Sonia still harbored the fear of running into friends or acquaintances of her family.

Other times, we sought out a café that wasn't too crowded and, seated across from one another, we would remain in silence, with nothing to say.

We scraped the bottom of the barrel, digging up old childhood memories, which we each tried to pack with as much color as possible, then we would plunge back into silence.

When we were in my new apartment with the garden court-yard, Sonia sat rigidly for hours on a chair or in the only easy chair. That wasn't *her* home. It would be meaningless to move around in it.

But this wasn't the Sonia I'd fallen in love with.

I had pursued the myth of that unattainable sea creature garbed in silver, and I had lost myself in a very specific vision.

I was in love with the elegant, slightly distant figure that moved harmoniously, with an age-old naturalness, through the hallways and rooms of the house of the three girls, the house with its "private moon," the apartment that had become our home.

I had pursued a queen, and now I possessed a humble slave girl.

This new and bewildered Sonia had few of the features that had made me desire her so ardently. And now, all that remained to us even of sex was the mechanical ritual.

Yes, I know, Sonia had given me everything, but then she took everything away again.

Though that, I assure you, was not the reason I stopped loving her.

The pearl and the oyster, Gherardo's image was the one that came closest to the truth.

At the time, though, I believed it was only a problem that concerned Sonia and her family, in other words, a problem with Sonia's basic nature. Now, however, I discovered to my amazement that it had to do with me as well.

Taken out of her arabesque setting, Sonia no longer meant anything to me either. I too had chosen the pearl and the oyster, and now I found myself empty-handed.

# CHAPTER TWENTY-THREE

One afternoon, as I sat slouched in my easy chair, struggling to solve on my own the mystery of *The Murder of Roger Ackroyd*, Ruben phoned me.

"I have to talk to you right away, meet at the usual place," he said to me in a voice fraught with anxiety.

How can I ever forget that afternoon, with the Agatha Christie book lying open, and how I started walking downstairs, down and down toward the last step. I couldn't have imagined that that day there would be yet another step down, a step down to the underworld. I thought I'd walked down all the steps there were.

The "usual place" was at the intersection next to a newsstand, right before the street turned downhill. That was where Ruben and I generally met.

"It's Lorenza!" Ruben said to me without preamble. "They arrested almost her entire group at the university."

"What about her? Did they arrest her?" Perhaps it was a stupid question. If they had arrested Lorenza too, it would have been the first thing Ruben would have told me. All the same, I needed to hear some reassuring words.

"No, they didn't arrest her. Not for now . . . But you can imagine what Lorenza is feeling. At a single blow, the only solid point of reference in her life has been swept away, her sole reason for hope. Her commitment, her group, her friends . . ."

I asked Ruben if he thought that she was still in danger, if they might be planning to arrest Lorenza in a second sweep.

"I doubt it, it's been three days . . ."

But while Ruben spoke to me, engrossed in the details, as if he were thinking aloud, I sensed a surge of something that felt like a mixture of pain and grief and a stab of unbridled jealousy. How could this be!? Three days had gone by, and I was being told about it only now? I really must no longer be part of Lorenza's life, I was cut out of it all, to a much greater degree than was right, much more than I would have wanted. Ruben . . .

"We waited to tell you because we wanted to see how it would turn out. We spent days holding our breath. Yes." Ruben was answering a question that I hadn't asked him, but had certainly thought: "Yes, we started seeing one another again, I couldn't just leave her alone. Who do you think she could have turned to?"

Sure, who did I think she could have turned to . . . Could she have turned to me, the great recluse, the one who had stepped out of history once and for all?

"What a relief they didn't arrest her," I murmured at this point in a flat voice.

"Doesn't it strike you as odd, though? What do you think?" Ruben also maintained the distracted tone of voice of someone intently following a logical thread.

"Oh, the police often get things wrong, they miss important details . . ."

"Don't you think her family might have had something to do with this?" Ruben blurted out, finally raising his eyes to meet mine.

Could her family, could "they" have known about all this from the very beginning? Could they have waited in the shadows, allowing Lorenza to act, ready to swoop down and intervene when the time was right? And so the canary felt free and independent in her big cage, unaware the whole time that bars surrounded her, that she was in a cage all right, but just didn't know it?

No, no matter how much I hated "them," I couldn't bring myself to believe it. It was too contrived, out of keeping with someone who certainly knew how to unleash a crushing onslaught when he wanted to, but, all things considered, did so directly, face-to-face.

Ruben didn't think so either. What he thought was that someone very highly placed, seeing that name and investigating the individual in question, had found out who Lorenza was related to, and had discreetly alerted the family. And of course, the family had "taken care of things," the fix was in. Which, after all, was not so very different from the more serious hypothesis.

And it all happened without a word to Lorenza. It would have been too risky, given her personality.

"Doesn't it strike you as a remarkable coincidence that, without the slightest reason to do so, Signora Adelaide asked Lorenza to come with her to tour the Venice Biennale? Now, of all times, when Lorenza is about to take her exams?"

Yes, perhaps it was a little odd, but not all that strange. "They" lived a comfortable life, and they enjoyed filling their days with enjoyable events, perhaps to help them forget the more unpleasant things.

"Does Lorenza suspect anything?" I finally asked, and Ruben explained that this time Lorenza was as far as could be imagined from any thoughts of the sort. Perhaps it was because she was overwhelmed by the anguish of losing so many friends, so many fellow militants at one fell swoop, and she was too concerned about their fate to worry about anything else. She hadn't had time to think about herself and her own situation.

"Will she go?" I shouted after Ruben, who was moving away practically at a run, because he realized he would be late for work.

"Go where?" Ruben shot back in amazement.

"Go to Venice, of course."

"Are you joking? She wouldn't dream of it," Ruben said, and hurried off after waving goodbye with one hand.

*

When I finally saw Lorenza, she seemed, understandably, more beaten down than ever. The way she moved, the way she talked made me think of someone else, not her, but an older relative from whom she had inherited some vague resemblance.

She told me, with a wealth of detail, what she had heard about the arrests—or perhaps we should say, the mass arrest—of her group. For the first time, she told me about a certain Luisa, and their ideological leader, Giovanni, about how and where they printed their leaflets, how they distributed them, often by slipping them into mailboxes directly, thus eluding the notice of concierges—whether they liked it or not, the Fascist regime had transformed the concierges of Italy into informers.

This was the first time that Lorenza had spoken to me openly about her political activity. Maybe she had assumed I knew before, but she had taken care not to make even the slightest reference to it.

"It's lucky they didn't come looking for you," I ventured, feeling my way over delicate ground.

"Yeah," Lorenza replied, lost in thought. "I don't know why. It doesn't strike me that I was any more cautious than the others."

Her tone of voice was open and sincere. Ruben had been right.

That her family might theoretically have intervened on her behalf had never even crossed Lorenza's mind.

That's good, I thought. Then I started scolding Lorenza for not having contacted me as soon as it happened. "The first I heard about it was three days later, from Ruben," I added, bitterly.

"Dino! You already have so many problems, a life in smithereens, and each of those smithereens shattered . . . Do you think I'd drop even worse things on you?"

A life in smithereens, shattered. That's how Lorenza saw me, that's what I looked like to the outside world. And Lorenza didn't consider me strong enough to help her; in fact, she thought of me as practically nonexistent.

So this was the truth. There was no point in trying to hide behind the cover of a murder mystery.

But what about her? Hadn't her life been blown into smithereens too? Was the Lorenza I knew the same as the one I watched as she walked slowly away from me, almost shuffling, her eyes gazing at the ground in loss?

It truly is a tragedy when life beats down a winner and manages to vanquish her. It was something I had thought before, and now it surfaced in my thoughts.

I wouldn't know till later how prophetic that thought had been.

Now comes the beginning of the nightmare. Sonia knocks at my door, pounding with both hands, not even bothering to ring the doorbell. When I open the door, she shouts: "Come on! It's Lorenza!"

"Lorenza?"

"Lorenza's had an accident," she shouts.

"What kind of accident?" I shout back at her.

"I'm not sure—a streetcar—she's been run over by a streetcar . . ."

"What?" I go on shouting. "She . . . she threw herself in front of a streetcar!?"

"Who said she threw herself? No one said she threw herself! It was an accident, it was an accident, I told you."

We run out and jump into Sonia's taxi, waiting by the curb with the motor running.

We drive quickly across the city and we pull up in front of a long, low building—the hospital.

*They're* all there, in the hallway, in front of a closed door, ashen-faced, gripping one another. It's *them*, the ones who devised the *plan*.

I ought to feel pity for them, but I can't bring myself to do so.

I feel as if they are looking at me with bewilderment and hostility, that my presence in that hospital corridor strikes them as incongruous, disturbing, out of place, but what do I care about them?

Sonia doesn't seem to care about what they think either, because she's been gripping my arm without letting go, clutching it spasmodically.

We all stare at one another without a word. The minutes go by as if they were hours.

From the windows lining that hospital corridor I see, behind the glass, a mimosa tree, swaying frivolously in the wind. What does that mimosa tree know about what's happening here, behind the glass? Frothy and yellow, it will continue to dance in the wind long after some of us are gone.

"She was so distracted lately . . . so tired . . . those damned exams were too tiring," moaned Signora Adelaide, unable to withstand the silence.

Of course, the exams. They had constructed that cage around her, until one day she realized it was there, because she had flown directly into the bars . . .

At that moment, I was overwhelmed by the certainty that Lorenza must suddenly have understood everything. Must have understood what Ruben and then I had thought from the very beginning, while she remained inexplicably oblivious to the possibility.

But how could I be sure of it? Maybe Sonia was right. It had been an accident and nothing more. Lorenza wasn't the sort of person who committed rash acts. Lorenza had said to me: "They took everything away from you." What if she had realized they'd done the same thing to her? Marriage, friends, ideas, political engagement. Now what was left to Lorenza? Of course . . . she still had her family. A family that was so good at "taking care" of things. They had taken care of things for me, and of course they'd be willing, even eager, to do the same thing for their daughter.

Time kept on passing, the mimosa tree kept on swaying, and all those specters gathered in that hallway kept on waiting.

But when the doctor opened that cursed door and emerged, shaking his head, I understood immediately that there was nothing left to wait for. I sensed that *they* had struck once again.

I don't know what drove me to what I did next. I don't even remember how I suddenly lunged at Giuseppe Gentile, how I seized him by the tie, tugging at him and punching him, shouting into his face: "You killed my sister! You killed my sister!"

Everyone was grabbing at me, trying to pull me off him . . . I think there were nurses in white smocks and I heard voices (further away or closer by?) calling out, "He's crazy, he's crazy!" But once I had released my grip on Giuseppe Gentile's throat, I managed to seize Sonia's arm, and I went on repeating to her, to Sonia, crushed by grief, yes, repeating to her in a suddenly calm and measured voice: "You killed my sister."

Then I allowed myself to be pushed outside.

From that day forward, I never again saw a single member of that family.

Absolutely no one.

I fled the way Cain fled, an exile . . . No, I fled the way Abel would have fled.

# CHAPTER TWENTY-FOUR

M ichele, I don't know if you have any memories of your aunt Lorenza. When she vanished forever from your life, you had just turned six, and they must have done everything within their power to keep you as far as possible from that tragedy.

Perhaps you can still remember a fragmentary image of an exuberant young woman who loved to play with you on the carpet in the Via Borgelli, or who took care of you and kept you company when your grandmother would take you away on holiday to Conero. But maybe time has wiped all that away . . .

I hope you can understand me, Michele. I never meant, by writing you these feverish pages, to deliberately destroy the image you might have of your mother's family. Do you think that while I have been crudely describing to you Sonia, Clotilde, Giuseppe Gentile, and his wife Adelaide, and finally Gherardo, that I ever forgot that I was talking about your mother, your aunt, your grandparents, and your cousin, who may have truly and definitively become your father by now?

I had no choice but to do this. Believe me, I never wanted to "open your eyes," as the expression goes. Quite the opposite.

You must have realized, I feel certain, that having a gentle and harmonious (yes, harmonious, let me say it one last time) person like your mother at your side is a rare privilege, and that Gherardo, whatever role he may now play in your life, is a man of lucid intelligence, free of all detritus of banality, and that your grandparents—I imagine that they are both dead by now—

must have been affectionate to you, as dear to you as they were to the rest of their family.

I ask your forgiveness for the sinister light in which I have depicted them to you. If you were still a boy, as I told you, I would never have expressed myself in these terms. But you're a grown man now, since you've already turned thirty-five, and so I have taken the liberty to assume that you could follow me. That you could come onto my territory. That you could understand me.

I never told anyone anything about my past during this long period of exile: or perhaps it wasn't exile, perhaps it was a coming ashore to a different life. I concealed my past even from myself. I buried it beneath a barren land, where so many—too many—others buried their memories to build something new.

I sincerely believed that I had succeeded in doing so.

Then came that sort of resurrection I described to you, in the first few days, when the pen began to move across sheet after sheet of paper, as if by a will of its own.

The feeling of having survived, victoriously, a threat of a new and different kind of extermination gave me a sudden sense of myself.

Suddenly, I felt within myself a sort of physical sensation, as if deep within me those waves of communication were reverberating, those waves that were sweeping across the sea, rapid and luminous. In both directions. Seeking and being sought.

I felt that I absolutely had to find my way back to you. That I too finally had to cross back over the sea.

I cautiously tried to jostle my memory, hoping that something, asleep for all these years, might flutter into wakefulness.

It happened. First, there was a cautious and awkward effort, then the whole flock burst into flight. My past began to be reborn, reborn for you.

I've told you everything, who I was, what and how I made my choices—or let others make choices on my behalf—my grim leaden errors, my hidden, masked suffering, my disheveled and merciless redemption.

Judge me as you wish.

But in order to allow you to judge me, I had to bring to *your* eyes the light of a harsh reality, a reality seen from *my* point of view, a reality in which your mother is only the loved-unloved Sonia and your grandparents appear as my implacable tormentors.

Lorenza's death (it's still harsh even now to attach such an inexorable word to describe her) brought a definitive end to the circle of my suffering. It struck a blow, as if an earthquake had pulled me out of the bout of self-pity in which I had chosen to wallow for those many long months.

I've always thought that Lorenza gave me this last gift. That even at the cost of allowing it to flicker out within herself, she succeeded in passing me the torch of her personal strength.

At last I had bellowed, at last I had hated.

At last I had abandoned everything and everyone.

Was my reaction cruel? Of course it was, that is self-evident. My revolt burst forth at the precise moment that the entire family was suffering most deeply: do you believe that the rational part of me was oblivious to that fact?

But hatred is a passion that moves terribly quickly because, unlike love, it need waste no time seeking a soulmate.

By now I was far away.

I was leaving Sonia, the woman I could no longer bring myself to love (or had our love been an illusion from the very beginning?), but I was also freeing Sonia.

I was no longer the brilliant young scholar who had helped her to open her mind to the world of ideas, I was no longer her invincible inamorato, unwilling to surrender until he succeeds in storming the castle and rescuing his princess . . .

What would Sonia want with a reader of mystery novels?

What was Sonia supposed to do with the dismantled pieces of a man to whom she was bound now only by remorse and pity?

I was leaving my son.

He was my son, but I was no longer his father. Rose is a rose, by any other name, but a father who can't call himself "father" is only a hollow sound.

Outside of any reality and surprise of everyday life, outside of any standard classification, by now whenever I saw my son he and I would sit there, gazing at one another with mistrust and sadness, always in the same tea room, though now, as the season advanced, we no longer drank hot chocolate with whipped cream; instead we ate colorful gelatos topped with a bright-red cherry.

I had written a letter to Sonia. In it, I asked for forgiveness and bade her farewell. A farewell that sounded both definitive and immediate.

It was true, I wanted to disappear then and there, but life has its practical restrictions, and a man cannot fly away simply by spreading his wings and leaping up freely into the sky.

I had to make preparations. I hurried over to my garden apartment and threw into a suitcase a few essentials, or at least things I considered essential at the time, though I was surely mistaken. Then I called a taxi, and directed the driver to the far end of Rome; there I looked for a *pensione*.

There, in that rented room, with its bed draped with an orange cover, its painting depicting a female saint, her eyes rolling upward, and its sink with a leaky faucet, I spent the days while I prepared my escape.

I don't know when it was, while I was tormenting myself, suffering, racking my brains in search of a solution, that I felt that illumination coming on.

I could leave, I could become a pioneer in Palestine, far away, in the land of the Jews.

It was all so clear, so logical, so inevitable!

From that moment on, my quest shifted from the realm of the abstract and the mental to the plane of the practical. Now I was working to achieve a specific goal.

I got in touch with the Jewish Agency . . . documents, bureaucratic requirements, visas, permits . . .

Then came the time to say goodbye to those I loved, those from whom I had not hidden myself.

When I wasn't busy rushing around the city, I spent almost all my days at Ruben's house. I stayed there with him. I had to seek his forgiveness for not suffering for him, but almost solely for myself.

I hugged Ruben and in tears I begged him to do as I was doing, to leave for Palestine with me. After all, he had always felt so much more Jewish than me.

"We're young . . . in Palestine we can still try to accomplish something. Why do you want to stay here, to witness the spectacle of Hitler devouring Europe, with Mussolini tagging along, beginning with the Jews!"

Ruben just shook his head and told me that he didn't feel he could make a decision of any kind. It was obvious that Lorenza had taken with her all his strength, that her departure had robbed Ruben of any ability to take up arms against the slings and arrows of life.

Ruben was now a helpless fragment, a scarred and broken individual whom I was no longer capable of resuscitating.

I would meet my parents on the street or in a café, in any case always somewhere other than the Albergo della Magnolia. I was afraid that Sonia might go there in search of me, perhaps seeking nothing more than news of me from my parents. It would have been a terrible thing if Sonia chanced upon me. She thought I had long since left the country.

And after all, the Albergo della Magnolia in Tiberio's hands was dead to me.

I spoke quickly and urgently to my father and my mother (this wasn't the first time I had done something like this, as you know). I didn't explain much, but above all I begged them not to tell Sonia I was still in the city, nor—obviously—to tell her where I was.

Then I made them swear that never, never, never would they tell me anything about my family.

"I need you to make sure I never know anything about them," I told them, without hiding the pain this cost me.

"Not even about your son?" my mother asked, looking at me with supplicant, grieving eyes.

"Mama, I'm doing this for my son. It's best for me to vanish from his life, it's best to let him truly be free." While my mother was preparing a response, a counterargument, and as her eyes began to well up with tears, my father stopped her with a gesture.

I'll always remember that slow and solemn gesture, like a benediction. "It's up to him . . . he knows what he has to do," my father had said in a calm voice.

Suddenly I felt as if I were emerging from a dark tunnel. I had finally glimpsed a faint light. "He knows what he has to do," my father had said.

My father understood that I was regaining control of my life.

On the first of September of that terrible year, Germany invaded Poland. On the third of that month, France and England declared war on Germany. War. Europe was already at war.

My father had foreseen it. The same instinct had allowed him to guess that this war would be longer and more tragic than any war before it. My father had understood before anyone else, then gradually, watching Hitler's moves, I had understood what was coming, as had many many others by now.

When I told my parents that I was going to leave for Palestine, I saw that they had more or less been expecting it.

Palestine or South America: these were the paths that Jews took to flee, now that Europe was about to sunk in the flood.

Then I began my campaign of persuasion. I begged them to come with me, to join me later. They could come, certainly not to plow new farmland, but to set up housekeeping in some city. I never stopped asking them, never stopped demanding that they come, forcefully, obstinately. They could live in any city, any village, on the beach or among the dunes, anywhere, as long as they escaped the threat weighing on the heads of all the Jews of Europe. That threat about which my father had heard stories, so long ago, from the mysterious travelers who washed up, bewildered, scattered, in the kitchens of the Albergo della Magnolia.

As I told you at the beginning, I succeeded in persuading them. It was my one consolation, and it partly made up for all the pain of those shattered years.

Less than a year later, a few days before Italy declared war alongside Germany, my parents, having sold for a pittance the Albergo della Magnolia to Tiberio, were disembarking from a ship, completely bewildered and loaded down with trunks, crates, suitcases, memories, and homesickness, but finally free.

The ship had docked at the port of Haifa, in the land of the Jews.

I was there to meet them. To greet the only relatives I had managed to save.

Ruben was killed while he was fighting with the partisans in the Castelli Romani, outside of the city. Aunt Esterina, with her whole family, was rounded up by the Germans in a house where she had hoped they'd be safe, and shipped off in the boxcars of death, almost certainly to Auschwitz. Nothing more was ever heard of them. We never even knew where their ashes were scattered.

I had arrived in Palestine in the fall of the year before, and I was already battling the sand and rocks of the desert.

Let me tell you one more thing about my departure. I had already been ready for some time, but I wanted to wait for school to begin.

Concealed on the far side of the street, I watched you, Michele, you, my son, in your dark-blue smock, with a white collar and bow, enter school for the first day of your life as a student.

You were walking happily, holding your mother by the hand, your blond hair and Aryan features a picture that would have made Mussolini beam with pleasure.

For some time now my cat Shulamit has become more tractable; in other words, she's not so angry with me nowadays when she sees me bent over these sheets of paper.

Perhaps she senses that I've almost finished, and that the words I am writing now truly are the last lines.

Do you remember what I told you at the beginning? I confessed to you that I had felt inside me an irresistible urge to start pulling out and untangling the story of my past, ideally addressing it to you, though I was uncertain whether one day I would send it to you.

As you can see, I've changed my mind. After all, I am now convinced that the pages over which I have suffered, from a late fall to this hot summer, must reach you.

When you make a decision deep inside, it almost always seems to coincide mysteriously with some external event. That is, it almost always seems to be seconded by circumstance. For example, now I have an address to mail my letter to, which by now of course is no ordinary letter, but a very substantial folder of letters.

The other day, I saw a photograph of Gherardo. That's right, I happened to see him. Ever since I started thinking about the "other side," I buy an Italian newspaper now and again.

And there he was.

A photograph published in that newspaper depicted him toasting with a group of important people the inauguration of a state-of-the-art wine cellar built for the production of a new line of fine wines. In the article that accompanied the photograph, I read that for the occasion, Gherardo had even funded the restoration of a Tuscan castle from the thirteenth century.

I looked at the photograph for a long time. So many years have passed, but I recognized Gherardo immediately. He didn't strike me as any different. Then, one by one, I scrutinized the faces of all the members of the festive group. I wanted to see if you were there. There were one or two young men (one stood next to a lovely dark-haired girl), but how could I recognize you? Love alone, no matter what people may naïvely say, is not capable of acting as a prompter.

But now I know that the bulky envelope with your name on it will be mailed to Gherardo's address in the rolling Tuscan countryside, to that estate where grapevines and olive groves stretch out as far as the eye can see, from the hills to the plain.

I remember that estate, and I imagine that it alone has survived, as the land always survives, outliving the fickle whims of fate. I wonder if the Via Borgelli is still there. Still there for the family, I mean . . .

Michele, I don't know what's become of you. I don't know how Sonia, your mother, has acted, but whatever decision she made, I feel sure that she made it with wisdom and prudence.

I don't know whether Gherardo gradually became your real father; perhaps your memory of me has dwindled until it has been completely forgotten. After all, the last time you saw me, you had just turned six.

Or perhaps when the war ended they explained everything to you. And if they did, perhaps from time to time you thought about that lost father, who evaporated into history . . .

As for me, I think I hardly need tell you, that there hasn't been a day or a night, a season or a place that I didn't think intensely about you.

Some nights I can't sleep, or else I sleep and dream that I'm not sleeping. And all in a rush come those images, sometimes to torment me, other times to keep me company. And I see Sonia in her silvery gown, I see the beautiful and foolish Clotilde, and even the poor nurse with her bedraggled shoes, who took letters back and forth between Sonia and me.

But those are merely images that hover aimlessly in the air. By now the past has lost its dominion over my heart.

I never see you, though. You are too much a part of my thoughts and concerns to turn into a nocturnal phantom.

That's how life has gone.

There are period when history rules, when history dictates its iron laws. But there is one thing I've understood. There are many ways to obey those laws. Many ways to submit.

In those years, when "she," that is, history, gave orders, there were those who were warriors, others who were spies, some were ready to succumb and others were capable of seizing flashes of dignity.

After all, history does nothing more than to exasperate and place at center stage that which we really are, mixing and remixing the passions and darknesses that churn deep inside us. The endless array of human emotions and turmoil. What in peacetime might be no more than a simple compromise in the turbulent storms of wartime can easily become a betrayal. A betrayal that sends you to your death.

Same emotions, different tone. I wonder if you know what I mean.

I told you about the humiliating agreement that I entered into during my first meeting with Sonia's father. Well, for many years I believed that, if the race laws hadn't been issued, and then the war hadn't come, if Mussolini and Hitler hadn't happened to cross paths with all of us, that agreement of mine would have meant nothing, or close to it, it would have been a decision with very limited consequences.

Now I'm certain that's not how things work; I've grown to understand this while writing to you.

Everything that is dark within us is destined to reflect its opaque black outside of us as well—the black of a toxic flower that will take root in darkness and ultimately spew its poison.

Nowadays I believe that no matter what, in any circumstance, in any place, that agreement would have ultimately produced devastating consequences in our lives, even without the specter of lead-sealed boxcars.

That's why I've told you everything.

You are free to do as you like with what I have placed before your eyes. You may suffer, hate, accept or reject, understand, forgive or curse, or even perhaps love. Anything is possible.

But before you act, you need to have all the cards face up, in your hand.

Then you can make any decision you like. I chose not to exist. You must choose not to want.

The important thing is to be aware. Don't let your life be tossed back and forth by waves that break and splash with a will of their own.

That's enough preaching; I'm done with morals. I didn't write you to engage in rhetoric, much less sermons.

I merely entrusted the bottle to the waves.

Now that I have nothing left to write, I can only imagine, dream, fantasize, and construct pathetic scenarios, and then amuse myself by destroying them.

My heart is at peace, though, you know? I suddenly feel tranquil, and so I have decided to resume my translation of Pindar (don't laugh, I know that it's been something like thirty years). I feel a new enthusiasm in my heart for this ancient commitment.

In my nighttime imaginings, I see a young man climb aboard

an airplane, flying over the waters and disembarking, perhaps bewildered the way his grandparents once were, in this ancient land.

I am not asking you to really take that flight; I can only allow myself to build the scene inside my head, inside my heart.

I need to remind you of one more thing. When I described my apartment to you, I told you, I think, that it's not very big and it's not all that nice? However, if you come in, and you walk to the far end, and you lean over the little balcony, you can glimpse the sea.

Just lean out a little way, and you'll be able to glimpse the sea, I assure you.

## About the Author

Lia Levi is author of many books for adults and for children. She has been awarded the Elsa Morante First Novel Prize (1994) and the Moravia Prize (2001). For many years, she was the editor-in-chief of the Jewish monthly *Shalom*. She lives in Rome.

**Carmine Abate**
*Between Two Seas*
"A moving portrayal of generational continuity."—*Kirkus*
192 pp • $14.95 • 978-1-933372-40-2

**Salwa Al Neimi**
*The Proof of the Honey*
"Al Neimi announces the end of a taboo in the Arab world:
that of sex!"—*Reuters*
160 pp • $15.00 • 978-1-933372-68-6

**Alberto Angela**
*A Day in the Life of Ancient Rome*
"Fascinating and accessible."—*Il Giornale*
392 pp • $16.00 • 978-1-933372-71-6

**Muriel Barbery**
*The Elegance of the Hedgehog*
"Gently satirical, exceptionally winning and inevitably
bittersweet."—Michael Dirda, *The Washington Post*
336 pp • $15.00 • 978-1-933372-60-0

**Stefano Benni**
*Margherita Dolce Vita*
"A modern fable...hilarious social commentary."—*People*
240 pp • $16.95 • 978-1-933372-20-4

*Timeskipper*
"Benni again unveils his Italian brand of magical realism."—*Library Journal*
400 pp • $16.95 • 978-1-933372-44-0

**Massimo Carlotto**
*The Goodbye Kiss*
"A masterpiece of Italian noir."—*Globe and Mail*
160 pp • $14.95 • 978-1-933372-05-1

*Death's Dark Abyss*
"A remarkable study of corruption and redemption."
—*Kirkus* (starred review)
160 pp • $14.95 • 978-1-933372-18-1

*The Fugitive*
"[Carlotto is] the reigning king of Mediterranean noir."
—*The Boston Phoenix*
176 pp • $14.95 • 978-1-933372-25-9

**Francisco Coloane**
*Tierra del Fuego*
"Coloane is the Jack London of our times."—Alvaro Mutis
176 pp • $14.95 • 978-1-933372-63-1

**Giancarlo De Cataldo**
*The Father and the Foreigner*
"A slim but touching noir novel from one of Italy's best writers
in the genre."—*Quaderni Noir*
160 pp • $15.00 • 978-1-933372-72-3

**Shashi Deshpande**
*The Dark Holds No Terrors*
"[Deshpande is] an extremely talented storyteller."—*Hindustan Times*
272 pp • $15.00 • 978-1-933372-67-9

**Steve Erickson**
*Zeroville*
"A funny, disturbing, daring and demanding novel—Erickson's best."
—*The New York Times Book Review*
352 pp • $14.95 • 978-1-933372-39-6


**Elena Ferrante**
*The Days of Abandonment*
"The raging, torrential voice of [this] author is something rare."
—*The New York Times*
192 pp • $14.95 • 978-1-933372-00-6

*Troubling Love*
"Ferrante's polished language belies the rawness
of her imagery."—*The New Yorker*
144 pp • $14.95 • 978-1-933372-16-7

*The Lost Daughter*
"So refined, almost translucent."—*The Boston Globe*
144 pp • $14.95 • 978-1-933372-42-6

**Jane Gardam**
*Old Filth*
"Old Filth belongs in the Dickensian pantheon of memorable characters."—*The New York Times Book Review*
304 pp • $14.95 • 978-1-933372-13-6

*The Queen of the Tambourine*
"A truly superb and moving novel."—*The Boston Globe*
272 pp • $14.95 • 978-1-933372-36-5

*The People on Privilege Hill*
"Engrossing stories of hilarity and heartbreak."—*Seattle Times*
208 pp • $15.95 • 978-1-933372-56-3

**Alicia Giménez-Bartlett**
*Dog Day*
"Delicado and Garzón prove to be one of the more engaging sleuth teams to debut in a long time."—*The Washington Post*
320 pp • $14.95 • 978-1-933372-14-3

*Prime Time Suspect*
"A gripping police procedural."—*The Washington Post*
320 pp • $14.95 • 978-1-933372-31-0

*Death Rites*
"Petra is developing into a good cop, and her earnest efforts to assert her authority…are worth cheering."—*The New York Times*
304 pp • $16.95 • 978-1-933372-54-9

**Katharina Hacker**
*The Have-Nots*
"Hacker's prose soars."—*Publishers Weekly*
352 pp • $14.95 • 978-1-933372-41-9


**Patrick Hamilton**
*Hangover Square*
"Patrick Hamilton's novels are dark tunnels of misery, loneliness, deceit, and sexual obsession."—*New York Review of Books*
336 pp • $14.95 • 978-1-933372-06-8


**James Hamilton-Paterson**
*Cooking with Fernet Branca*
"Irresistible!"—*The Washington Post*
288 pp • $14.95 • 978-1-933372-01-3

*Amazing Disgrace*
"It's loads of fun, light and dazzling as a peacock feather."
—*New York Magazine*
352 pp • $14.95 • 978-1-933372-19-8

*Rancid Pansies*
"Campy comic saga about hack writer and self-styled 'culinary genius' Gerald Samper."—*Seattle Times*
288 pp • $15.95 • 978-1-933372-62-4

*Seven-Tenths: The Sea and Its Thresholds*
"The kind of book that, were he alive now, Shelley might have written."
—Charles Sprawson
416 pp • $16.00 • 978-1-933372-69-3

**Alfred Hayes**
*The Girl on the Via Flaminia*
"Immensely readable."—*The New York Times*
160 pp • $14.95 • 978-1-933372-24-2


**Jean-Claude Izzo**
*Total Chaos*
"Izzo's Marseilles is ravishing."—*Globe and Mail*
256 pp • $14.95 • 978-1-933372-04-4

*Chourmo*
"A bitter, sad and tender salute to a place equally impossible
to love or leave."—*Kirkus* (starred review)
256 pp • $14.95 • 978-1-933372-17-4

*Solea*
"[Izzo is] a talented writer who draws from the deep, dark well
of noir."—*The Washington Post*
208 pp • $14.95 • 978-1-933372-30-3

*The Lost Sailors*
"Izzo digs deep into what makes men weep."
—*Time Out New York*
272 pp • $14.95 • 978-1-933372-35-8

*A Sun for the Dying*
"Beautiful, like a black sun, tragic and desperate."—*Le Point*
224 pp • $15.00 • 978-1-933372-59-4

**Gail Jones**
*Sorry*
"Jones's gift for conjuring place and mood rarely falters."
—*Times Literary Supplement*
240 pp • $15.95 • 978-1-933372-55-6

**Matthew F. Jones**
*Boot Tracks*
"A gritty action tale."—*The Philadelphia Inquirer*
208 pp • $14.95 • 978-1-933372-11-2

**Ioanna Karystiani**
*The Jasmine Isle*
"A modern Greek tragedy about love foredoomed
and family life."—*Kirkus*
288 pp • $14.95 • 978-1-933372-10-5

**Gene Kerrigan**
*The Midnight Choir*
"The lethal precision of his closing punches leave quite a lasting mark."
—*Entertainment Weekly*
368 pp • $14.95 • 978-1-933372-26-6

*Little Criminals*
"A great story...relentless and brilliant."—Roddy Doyle
352 pp • $16.95 • 978-1-933372-43-3

**Peter Kocan**
*Fresh Fields*
"A stark, harrowing, yet deeply courageous work of immense power and magnitude."—*Quadrant*
304 pp • $14.95 • 978-1-933372-29-7

*The Treatment and the Cure*
"Kocan tells this story with grace and humor."—*Publishers Weekly*
256 pp • $15.95 • 978-1-933372-45-7

**Helmut Krausser**
*Eros*
"Helmut Krausser has succeeded in writing a great German epochal novel."—*Focus*
352 pp • $16.95 • 978-1-933372-58-7

**Amara Lakhous**
*Clash of Civilizations Over an Elevator in Piazza Vittorio*
"Do we have an Italian Camus on our hands? Just possibly."
—*The Philadelphia Inquirer*
144 pp • $14.95 • 978-1-933372-61-7

**Carlo Lucarelli**
*Carte Blanche*
"Lucarelli proves that the dark and sinister are better evoked
when one opts for unadulterated grit and grime."
—*The San Diego Union-Tribune*
128 pp • $14.95 • 978-1-933372-15-0

*The Damned Season*
"De Luca…is a man both pursuing and pursued. And that makes him one
of the more interesting figures in crime fiction."
—*The Philadelphia Inquirer*
128 pp • $14.95 • 978-1-933372-27-3

*Via delle Oche*
"Delivers a resolution true to the series' moral relativism."
—*Publishers Weekly*
160 pp • $14.95 • 978-1-933372-53-2

**Edna Mazya**
*Love Burns*
"Combines the suspense of a murder mystery with the absurdity
of a Woody Allen movie."—*Kirkus*
224 pp • $14.95 • 978-1-933372-08-2

**Sélim Nassib**
*I Loved You for Your Voice*
"Nassib spins a rhapsodic narrative out of the indissoluble
connection between two creative souls."—*Kirkus*
272 pp • $14.95 • 978-1-933372-07-5

*The Palestinian Lover*
"A delicate, passionate novel in which history and life are
inextricably entwined."—*RAI Books*
192 pp • $14.95 • 978-1-933372-23-5

**Amélie Nothomb**
*Tokyo Fiancée*
"Intimate and honest...depicts perfectly a nontraditional romance."
—*Publishers Weekly*
160 pp • $15.00 • 978-1-933372-64-8

**Alessandro Piperno**
*The Worst Intentions*
"A coruscating mixture of satire, family epic, Proustian meditation,
and erotomaniacal farce."—*The New Yorker*
320 pp • $14.95 • 978-1-933372-33-4

**Eric-Emmanuel Schmitt**
*The Most Beautiful Book in the World*
"Nine novellas, parables on the idea of a future, filled with redeeming
optimism."—*Lire Magazine*
192 pp • $15.00 • 978-1-933372-74-7

**Domenico Starnone**
*First Execution*
"Starnone's books are small theatres of action, both physical
and psychological."—*L'espresso* (Italy)
176 pp • $15.00 • 978-1-933372-66-2

**Joel Stone**
*The Jerusalem File*
"Joel Stone is a major new talent."—*Cleveland Plain Dealer*
160 pp • $15.00 • 978-1-933372-65-5

**Benjamin Tammuz**
*Minotaur*
"A novel about the expectations and compromises that humans
create for themselves."—*The New York Times*
192 pp • $14.95 • 978-1-933372-02-0

**Chad Taylor**
*Departure Lounge*
"There's so much pleasure and bafflement to be derived
from this thriller."—*The Chicago Tribune*
176 pp • $14.95 • 978-1-933372-09-9

**Roma Tearne**
*Mosquito*
"Vividly rendered…Wholly satisfying."—*Kirkus*
352 pp • $16.95 • 978-1-933372-57-0

*Bone China*
"Tearne deftly reveals the corrosive effects of civil strife
on private lives and the redemptiveness of art."—*The Guardian*
432 pp • $16.00 • 978-1-933372-75-4

**Christa Wolf**
*One Day a Year: 1960-2000*
"Remarkable!"—*The New Yorker*
640 pp • $16.95 • 978-1-933372-22-8

**Edwin M. Yoder Jr.**
*Lions at Lamb House*
"Yoder writes with such wonderful manners, learning,
and detachment."—William F. Buckley, Jr.
256 pp • $14.95 • 978-1-933372-34-1

**Michele Zackheim**
*Broken Colors*
"A beautiful novel."—*Library Journal*
320 pp • $14.95 • 978-1-933372-37-2